DEATH OF A STRANGER

DEATH OF A STRANGER

Eileen Dewhurst

This first world edition published in Great Britain 1999 by
SEVERN HOUSE PUBLISHERS LTD of
9–15 High Street, Sutton, Surrey SM1 1DF.
This first world edition published in the U.S.A. 1999 by
SEVERN HOUSE PUBLISHERS INC of
595 Madison Avenue, New York, N.Y. 10022.

British Library Cataloguing in Publication Data

Dewhurst, Eileen
        Death of a stranger
        1.   Detective and mystery stories
        I.   Title
        823.9'14 [F]

        ISBN 0-7278-2282-9

Typeset by Palimpsest Book Production Ltd
Polmont, Stirlingshire, Scotland.
Printed and bound in Great Britain by
MPG Books Ltd, Bodmin, Cornwall.

For Alf and Iola Sealey

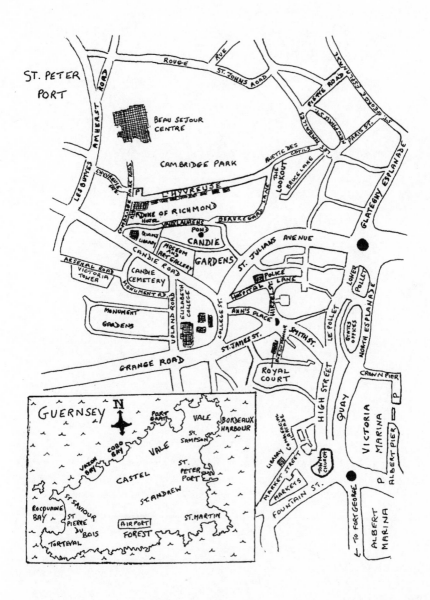

One

" Tim! My darling boy!"

She was wearing the same scent and he was no longer a detective inspector in the Guernsey police force, he was a child lying in bed and looking up in wonderment at the beautiful face bent over him, the sparkling drops to each side of it brushing his hair as the lips reached his cheek.

But he was the one, now, who must bend for their faces to make contact, and as he straightened up he smiled his long-suffering love for her.

"You really are pleased to see me, aren't you, darling?" His mother's tone to him was still the contented purr which turned what might be no more than a minute of her concentration into a sense of forever. "But I've always tended to get more than I deserve."

"Of course I am. And that scent . . . It's the same, isn't it?"

"Of course it is. I may not be faithful to my men, but I'm faithful to my perfume. Now, stand back and let me look at you . . ." For the few seconds that her wide eyes studied him, he was the whole of her life. "Yes, you're well and you're happy."

"That's it, Mother."

Studying her in his turn, Tim saw to his loyal relief that she continued to be beautiful. Perhaps even more beautiful to

1

his adult eye than she had been those intermittent times over the past decades when she had flown briefly in – always, it seemed to him, slightly breathless – to give him a few exciting, scent-filled hours of her company. The fine bones were if anything more pronounced and he found himself accepting, with another surge of relief, that she was moving towards a lean old age which would enable her to look like herself until her end. As always, she was dressed with quiet perfection, a scarlet wisp of scarf at the neck of her immaculate white blouse, her bare brown legs, visible from the knee down, as long and slender as when he had first been aware of them.

But the usual hint of shared fun had left her face, and she was looking at him now with uncharacteristic hesitancy. As he noted the change Tim also noted, with a stab of disappointment that was dismally familiar, that she was without a trolley, and that the tall, fair young man in charge of one who had come to a halt behind her was up to his chest in piled luggage.

"Darling . . . This is Simon. Simon – Shaw. A friend from London. He's got business on the island and so we decided to travel together. I rang the Duke when I knew he was coming and managed to get him a room. Simon, this is my son Tim."

"Hello." The young men spoke in unison as they looked at one another.

"Be nice to Simon, Tim," his mother said. She spoke lightly, but this hardly dispelled Tim's uneasy surprise that she should bother to ask such a favour of him, it was so unlike her usual airy presentation of her current male attachment. "He's my good friend."

"I see." There had been a slight emphasis on the last word, and Tim found himself yearning for it to be the truth. Despite his mother's long-term abdication of her roles as wife and mother he had retained his respect for her as well as his affection, and Simon Shaw was so very much junior to the youngish men she usually had in tow he hated the thought that he could be her lover. He didn't know whether or not to be reassured by the anxiety which was struggling through Shaw's formal smile: it could equally well indicate discomfort in so ludicrous a role as a wish for Tim to accept that he really was no more than a travelling companion.

"May I ask what your business here is?" he heard himself saying, trying not to be distracted by his strange realisation that in other circumstances he would have liked the look of Simon Shaw. "I'm not asking as a policeman." He managed a smile, and saw with a pang of pity his mother's gratitude.

"I appreciate that. But my business is confidential so I'm afraid I can't talk about it."

"I understand." *Only too well*, Tim continued cynically in his head. The odds had to be very short that the job Simon Shaw couldn't talk about didn't exist, and he had come to Guernsey because Lorna Le Page had taken a lover so young she was unable to acknowledge him.

"I'm sorry," the boy was saying again. He had an attractive voice, low and soft. He had turned to Lorna as he spoke, and although Tim read affection in his face he couldn't see desire. But his mother's behaviour had always been in good taste even while it had been outrageous, and she would have schooled him.

"There's no need to be sorry for having confidential business." It was an effort to carry on the chat. "Look," he said, turning to his mother, "let's get you to the hotel. The usual mountain of luggage, I see."

"Of course, darling. But so easy in Guernsey! Instant recovery, no crowds, loads of trolleys. Sarnian civilisation starts

3

the moment one lands and makes me wonder why I ever go away."

"You go away because you discovered years ago that the island was too small to contain you. Now, the car's in the park. Wait there and I'll bring it to the door." Tim turned to the boy. "You haven't hired yourself a car?" he heard himself ask, pointedly.

"I have. But Lorna suggested . . ." Tim was surprised to see fear in Simon Shaw's eyes as he looked to Tim's mother for support.

"Lorna suggested it should be delivered to the hotel, seeing that you were coming to collect me at the airport, darling," she took up swiftly. "No point in our leaving here in two cars when we can fit into one."

"Fine." There was nothing else to say. When he drove up Shaw was ready to load and went at it so briskly Tim merely tucked his mother into the front passenger seat, wondering if the man was being himself or trying to make a good impression. On the way to the hotel Shaw sat silent in the back while Lorna lauded the lush summer landscape.

"So you're well?" Tim asked, when she paused for breath.

"I think so. I don't really bother. Darling, I'm so dying to meet your Anna."

"And she you." Tim thought this was true. "She wanted to make a meal for us tonight" – *the three of us* – "but I persuaded her you would both enjoy your meeting better if it took place over a dinner table where someone else was doing the cooking. So I booked a table at the Duke." In view of the presence of Simon Shaw, Tim was sorry he had prevailed over Anna's expressed wish to prepare her first meal with her future mother-in-law herself, at home in Rouge Rue. Dining at the hotel they would feel obliged to invite the boy to join

4

them, and a stranger ambiguously connected with his mother would not help the beginnings of the relationship between the two women in Tim's life who were important to him. But he should have been ready for that stranger, Tim thought on a flare of anger, he shouldn't have expected a woman still as nubile and magnetic as his mother to travel alone, even to her son's marriage.

"And a table for three can become a table for four with a mere extra place setting." Tim was amused at the same time as he was troubled, by the mixture of statement and entreaty in his mother's voice. "Simon will be dining at the hotel, of course, and I'm sure Anna—"

"He must join us." Tim hoped he hadn't sounded as reluctant as he felt. And his mother *had* said she had booked another room. Knowing he would be unlikely to find an excuse for checking up . . .

For the time being at least, he must snap out of it.

"I'll leave you now," he said as he drew up outside the Duke of Richmond Hotel. "And Anna and I will present ourselves in the Saumarez Cabin bar at seven." He looked at his watch. "Only an hour and a half away and I haven't finished yet at the office, so I must dash."

"Thank you for inviting me to join you tonight." The boy had appeared beside him as he opened the boot. "I wasn't expecting to."

"No, well . . ."

"I just – look after her, Tim."

"Sure." He wanted to believe it. For the boy's sake as well, he realised with surprise. "So try to see she's in the Saumarez Cabin by seven."

"Will do. Thanks." Simon Shaw took the two largest cases in either hand and set off up the steps to the hotel door. Lorna, as always, was making no attempt to get out of the car on her own, and by the time Tim had opened her door and helped her on to the pavement Shaw had returned for the rest of the cases and there was nothing left for Tim to carry. And nothing overtly disturbing for him in the way his mother tucked her arm through the boy's as they made their way up the steps, or the way she smiled at him as he held the door for her . . .

Tim plunged back into the car, desperately wanting to be reassured and trying to tell himself that his mother's behaviour *vis-à-vis* Simon Shaw was of a different order from her behaviour *vis-à-vis* the other men in whose company she had returned over the years to Guernsey.

Would his mother be living faithfully still with Geoffrey Lorimer, Tim wondered as he drove the short steep way down to Town, if he hadn't died of a heart attack a few months after they had run away to England? And the embittered Constance, the wife he had fled from who, three decades on, still turned aside when she encountered Tim, would she want to confront the woman who in enduring local legend had ruined her life?

Not, please heaven, at his and Anna's wedding, although that would be the one occasion during his mother's short visit when Constance would know where to find the woman who had taken her place . . .

Tim was glad to find a small and easily-resolved crisis awaiting him at the station, acute enough for half an hour to force him to put his speculations on hold. But when he had raced up the steep stairs of his villa in Rouge Rue and found Anna getting ready for the evening, they came back to him.

"I hope Constance Lorimer keeps herself to herself while my mother's here," he mused aloud, when Anna had finished lamenting how much time it took her to free herself of the smell of the surgery before she could start taking positive steps to dress up.

"You said she was a timid soul and that could have been why your mother was able to court her husband and carry him off."

"Yes. But she's had years to brood and work my mother up in her mind into the ultimate Jezebel."

"Years could work the other way. Make her feel what the hell now, I can't be bothered."

"I suppose so. She still ignores me if we're within hailing distance."

"That could be for your sake as much as for hers. Tim, how do I look? Do you think your mother will approve of me? However carefully I do my hair, I'm still a woman who's only just got her decree absolute."

"Which may well prepare her to feel at home with you, given her own far more spectacular career." Tim moved across to his beloved, put his hands on her shoulders, and gazed at the pale, fine-featured face in its small frame of short, shining dark hair. "Thirty-six hours will be enough for her. To find out that she likes you," Tim added, seeing the teasing query in Anna's eyes. "Outside of male/female relationships, she's pretty reliable at getting it right. Anna . . ." Thinking about Constance Lorimer had made him forget about Simon Shaw. "I said in a jokey kind of a way that it was on the cards that even for my wedding my mother might bring a man with her. She has done."

"If you knew it was on the cards you shouldn't look so stricken, Tim. Is there something different?"

"Yes. He's really young. Half her age, I should say. And she rather went out of her way to tell me they were just good friends. And that he has business on the island. But when I asked him what that business was he said it was confidential and he couldn't tell me. But if Mother knows, I'll get it out of her. At least he doesn't look like a gigolo."

"How does a gigolo look?"

"Stop it. I don't know. But I think you'll know what I mean when you meet him. I found myself agreeing with Mother that we couldn't leave him to eat alone so I'm afraid he's of the party tonight. At least I got the impression that he's unlikely to push himself. And Mother wouldn't let him, anyway, on an occasion like tonight's; despite her lifestyle she has a sense of fitness."

"So don't worry, Tim. The things that matter are all right." She smiled her reassurance as she looked up from fastening a bracelet. "Now, you'd better get a move on."

They shut the front door on a reproachful dog, and walked to the Duke of Richmond through the soft, warm evening. Up the steep slope of Rouge Rue between serrations of villas as small and stout as Tim's and skyscapes of Edwardian chimney-pots, then as short a way as possible along the Amherst Road before turning off to cross the grassy edge of Cambridge Park and emerge in front of the hotel at the top of L'Hyvreuse.

Temporarily blinded by the change from light to dark as they entered the intimate red gloom of the Saumarez Cabin, Tim was vividly reminded of their entry one icy night at the beginning of the year to celebrate the fiftieth birthday of the senior partner in the veterinary practice where Anna was the junior, which had been their unwitting entry on a series of events that had almost cost Anna her life. The nightmare was so totally over it was hard to believe that less than six months had passed since it began, but Tim gave an involuntary shiver as he took Anna's hand. He had been slightly nervous on that earlier occasion, being brought in as the junior partner's lover, and he was slightly nervous again now, bringing his fiancée to meet his mother . . .

"Anna! Oh, just as I hoped!"

The tiny Saumarez Cabin was all alcoves, so there was nothing significant in the fact of his mother and Shaw sitting together in one of them. His mother had got to her feet and was advancing towards Tim and Anna, arms outstretched.

"Hello, Lorna." Anna put her arms out too, so that their hands met and clasped. By the light of the red lamp at the end of the bar counter, Tim saw an extra sparkle in his mother's eyes.

"Come and sit down!" Lorna commanded, retaining one of Anna's hands and drawing her towards the alcove. "This is such an important moment for me. Tim temperamentally is unlike me, you see, he's like his father. The same today as yesterday and tomorrow."

Feeling uncomfortably and uncharacteristically emotional, Tim noted his mother's pleased reaction to Anna's rare smile. "This is Simon Shaw," he told her, to distract himself and because Shaw was standing there so quiet and patient. Tim thought he saw something sorrowful in the boy's face – regret that he had no real part in a family celebration? – but as he met Tim's eyes he shyly smiled. "A friend of Mother's who's come over with her because he has business on the island." He could only paraphrase what they had both told him, and he was relieved to see Lorna nod her approval. "Now. Drinks."

When he got to the bar after taking their orders he discovered that Simon Shaw had signed an open chit. Another departure from his mother's usual boyfriends, none of whom Tim had ever seen so much as attempting to override her generosity. Although it could, of course, be no more than a PR exercise if his mother was ultimately paying the bills.

But he must acknowledge it. "I've just discovered that these are on Simon," he said, as he doled out the glasses. "Thank you, Simon." As he raised his, Tim saw a look pass between Simon Shaw and his mother that he could only define as satisfied complicity, and his sense of unease returned. The exchange had been without overt sexual content, but he had a few moments' work to discipline his fears and not allow them to obtrude on one of the most important evenings of his life. Simon Shaw was sharing it, there was nothing he could do about that. And his mother's attention, from then on and during dinner, was on Anna as she made it obvious how happily she was embracing his choice of bride. Not that it would have made a jot of difference if she had disliked Anna, Tim reflected unfilially, but her approval was a bonus to his still incredulous joy that Anna had chosen *him*, as was his slower realisation as the evening progressed that she was captivated by his mother's beguiling charm and obvious good intentions.

The wedding reception was to be at the hotel, and there was a flower arrangement on their table that was a happy earnest of how it would be adorned. Tim wondered if it was that or their patent air of celebration which had neighbouring diners smiling at them, then decided it was the presence of his mother who, with her recent and uncelebrated sixtieth birthday, had lost nothing of her unique charisma. He managed quite well during the dinner not to think too precisely about Simon Shaw – and Shaw's own quiet behaviour helped to make that easy – but he was aware of what he found himself defining as a proprietorial element in the boy's obvious enjoyment of Lorna's company which intrigued him at the same time as it evoked in him, to

10

his shocked astonishment, a pang of jealousy. Who the hell was Simon Shaw, to be regarding his, Tim's, mother as if he was her manager?

He was being fanciful, he had to be. It was only because Shaw didn't conform to his mother's usual sexual scenario. And it was so long since he had seen her, anyway, he'd probably forgotten what that scenario was; it wasn't a side of her life he had ever chosen to dwell on.

When they were sitting over their coffee Shaw asked them if they would excuse him, he had some paperwork to do before embarking the next morning on the work that had brought him to Guernsey, and he wanted to break the back of it before going to bed. "Thank you all so much for this evening, I've enjoyed it."

Shaw bent to kiss Lorna's cheek before leaving the table, and watching her face as the tall, fair-haired figure swung across the dining-room, Tim saw yearning in it and gave up his struggle to persuade himself that Simon Shaw was no more to his mother than a travelling companion.

"Mother's really attached to that boy," he said reluctantly to Anna as they came down the hotel steps into the windless, starry night.

"Yes, she is. Tim, I think we should ask him to the wedding. I think we've seen enough of him not to be afraid he'll take that as an invitation to sit with the bridal party."

"If he tried to, Mother would go mad. As I've told you probably too often, she has a sense of fitness."

"I saw it. Tim . . ." She held him back as he started across the road. "I've been to the lookout since I was attacked there after Brian's birthday party, but not at night. Can we go there now? I'm ready."

Eileen Dewhurst

"Good," Tim said, after studying her grave face in the light
streaming from the hotel lobby. "Come on, then."

Anna ran her arm through his as they started along
L'Hyvreuse. "How wise and wonderful of you to have
been able to take your mother on her own terms even when
you were small and keep her as a friend for life."

"That wasn't down to me in the early days. Darling Mother
never spelled security to me, as I've told you, that came from
my father and my grandmother – Mother's mother, believe it
or not, who used to tell me when I got older that she sometimes
suspected her daughter of being a changeling. So when Mother
left and Grandma moved in I'd lost a marvellous, glamorous
companion, not my lynchpin. I suppose it's strange, thinking
about it now, but I never blamed her, never felt she'd let me
down. When Father or Grandma told me she was coming to
see us I was so thrilled I could hardly wait."

"What a disappointment you'd be to a psychiatrist." Anna
found it strange, too, that she should be feeling a slight sense
of envy of Tim's unorthodox relationship with his mother.
Perhaps it was because, with her own mother's early death, she
had never had a chance to discover what sort of relationship
would have been possible between them. She had loved her
father but not her stepmother, and had left home as soon as
she could to live independently – which might account for the
slightly protective feeling that was constantly with her for the
more sheltered Tim, a feeling she would never reveal to him.

"In fact I had a very sheltered childhood." He looked at her
as they passed a street light. "Why are you smiling?" Anna's
face in repose was serious, and he had discovered that she
smiled only with reason.

"Because I'm happy." It wasn't a lie, she was as happy as
she had ever been. She had married Jimmy as a kind friend

12

who had comforted her when her first love had deserted her, and had known within days the dreadful wrong she had done them both. Their son had kept them together as baby and child, but when he was killed on the road she had left her husband, resumed work as a vet, and re-embraced her independence. Now Jimmy had found his true love she could have enjoyed that independence conscience-free, and even after she had told Tim she would marry him she had waited, her soul shivering, in terror of discovering that she was unable to let it go. But the discovery she had made was that Tim and independence were compatible and that with him she would be more her own woman than she would ever be on her own . . .

"All right?" Tim was asking cautiously.

"It makes remembering a bit too easy, but yes, it's all right."

They had reached the place where the attack had come, the wide low stone wall marking the end of L'Hyvreuse. St Peter Port was spread out below them, stabbed with sharp points of light beyond the immediate descent of old houses which was an impressionist jumble of soft smeared colours. The outlines of Herm and Sark were scarcely distinguishable from the unclouded sky, but the base of each island was defined by a blurred line of lights at the water's edge.

They stood in a silence to match the silence surrounding them, Anna routing her bad memories with Tim's hand over hers where it rested on the brass direction dial which, from her first days on the island staying at the Duke, she knew almost by heart. 'London 180, Alderney 21 . . .' It was only when below them a door opened and shut and voices began laughing and talking that, still silent, they turned away and started back up the hill.

The cat was sitting patient and upright against the front door, and the dog was hurling himself, breathing noisily, against the far side of it. They changed places as Tim pushed the door open, and by the time he and Anna were inside Duffy had danced three lengths of the short path to the gate and back, and the cat was prowling round the fridge.

"We've got to go away, haven't we?" Tim said, as Anna opened it and took out some catfood. "With our home life already under way there's nothing else to mark the arrival of Anna Le Page."

"I'd be happy enough just to come back here after the celebrations even so. But I'm glad we're going."

"And not regretful that it isn't anywhere exotic?"

"I asked you for Scotland. Are *you* sorry?"

"Of course not. I've never been, and for me it's abroad. How difficult it must have been once," Tim thought aloud, as they snuggled down in bed a half-hour later, trying to confine the cat to a bottom corner, "to have the fun of new places on a honeymoon all mixed up with having to adjust to going to bed together and, well . . ."

"I know. And not to be able to say 'Not tonight' for fear of irreparably damaging your new partner's feelings. Not tonight, my dearest darling, I'm asleep already."

"Me too." But although he dropped off almost at once, Tim's sleep was beset by dreams in which he prowled the thin byways of St Peter Port, looking for his mother but seeing only the distant figures of Simon Shaw and Constance Lorimer and never being able to catch them up.

Two

To give themselves a few unfevered hours in Lorna's company, Anna and Tim had devised the run-up to their wedding to allow for the completion of their preparations a day short of it, and their colleagues had insisted they finish work at lunchtime on Friday. Neither of them of course had the sort of job where this could be guaranteed, but Anna had kept her diary free of afternoon visits and Tim's one all-day concern was uninvolving enough for him to be quite easily persuaded to leave it in the hands of his sergeant.

So when he arrived home just before two o'clock he found his mother and his bride-to-be under the one big tree in his narrow walled garden, drinking coffee.

"Now, Mother," he said, when he had changed into a short-sleeved shirt and joined them for the second time, mug in hand, "what's this about your young friend Simon's job being so hush-hush we can't be told a thing about it?" She knew him as well as he knew her, and he wasn't sure he had been able to fool her that his question was light hearted.

Her eyes met his without blinking. "It is hush-hush, darling. But I've told him how utterly discreet you are and he's given me permission to tell you about it if I feel that maybe you're thinking that it doesn't exist. And that's what you are thinking, isn't it?"

Discomfited but at the same time reassured, Tim looked down at his knees.

"There you are, you see. But what Simon's more worried about telling you is what he is, with you being a policeman." Tim drew a sharp breath, and Anna got to her feet. "Look, I'll leave you both—"

"Please don't go, Anna," Lorna said. "Simon isn't ashamed of his profession, he just felt – well, I think he's afraid despite all my reassurances that Tim might look down on him."

"Would that matter?" Tim asked, immediately wishing he hadn't.

"I'll ignore that remark, darling," Lorna responded with dignity. "Simon's a private detective, he runs an agency in London, and he's been hired by an insurance company to carry out an undercover investigation over here. I gather the Guernsey branch manages most claims on its own but when something – well, something a weeny bit dubious – comes along, they consult their London office, and this time London took it seriously enough to hire Simon."

"Quite a responsibility for someone so young." Tim said it lightly, leaning up to pluck the bottom pair of leaves of the overhead ash frond as he spoke.

"He's had a lot of experience."

"I'm not doubting it. How did you and he meet, Mother?"

"He's the son of my friend Gina." For the first time since they had started talking about Shaw, her eyes slid away from his. But it could be simply because with what she was telling them she was fastening Shaw more securely into a younger generation. "You remember Gina, darling. Well, you remember hearing about her. Her husband was a distant cousin of Geoffrey's but not nearly so nice, in fact he was really foul to her and she had to ditch him."

16

"You seem to have had a few friends in that position."

"I do, darling, don't I? You'd like Gina, though, you both would, she's so amusing and articulate."

"Does she have other children?"

"Only Simon. All right?" Lorna dropped her eyes and started fiddling with the gilded chain that hung in the neck of her minimal turquoise top, beginning to look mutinous.

Anna decided to switch the line of questioning. "Simon's assignment sounds intriguing, Lorna. Can you really tell me as well as Tim about it?"

Lorna looked up, smiling her approval. "Of course. I can see already that you're as discreet as he is. It's the fire that destroyed a rose grower's greenhouse last month near Beaucette Marina. The Golden Rose." Tim and Anna murmured their recognition. "It must have been all over the *Guernsey Press* because of the valuable paintings in a cupboard inside the greenhouse. They'd been thought to be by some minor Florentine master – I can never remember which – and what with the high cost of the insurance and a couple of recent art thefts on the island . . ." Lorna looked a question at Tim, who nodded humbly. "Anyway, they'd decided to sell, and consulted a self-styled art expert friend who promptly called the pictures into question. So they made an appointment with a professional expert in town, for a few days after the fire. It isn't easy for a greenhouse to go up in smoke, which is one of the reasons the insurance company's uneasy, but it was very hot the day this one did, and the owners are saying that if the fire wasn't lit deliberately it must have been caused by a magnifying glass left by their son on top of some paper on a table near the cupboard – that particular greenhouse wasn't used for growing roses, the family used to eat and sit there in the summer, and the boy used the end where the pictures were as a sort of study, reading and doing his homework there. The fire happened on the one day in the week when the nursery closes, and the owners and their son had gone out. So the greenhouse was locked, but as most of the glass shattered in the heat there's no way of discovering if anyone had broken in and started the fire. And no sign inside of what might have started it apart from the remains of the magnifying glass. Someone saw the fire before it had time to spread to other buildings or really get the trees and bushes going, but it was too late to save either the greenhouse or the pictures."

"A strange place to store valuable pictures," Tim commented, lazy and detached. Sprawling in his peaceful garden and looking at the two women he loved, he had a moment of contentment so complete he knew it was happening and must be savoured there and then as well as in retrospect.

"Apparently not. The greenhouse was warm and dry and the wooden cupboard insulated them from any extremes of weather. And after the art thefts the owners felt the pictures would be safer there than in the house if the wrong people got wind of them. And it wasn't to be for long. If their knowledgeable friend hadn't cast doubt on them they'd probably have been sold by now."

"Or there might not have been a fire," Tim said.

"Or the insurance company would have paid out," Anna suggested.

"The insurance company may still pay out," Lorna said, yawning. "It depends on Simon's report."

"His report could be bringing me into the picture, if it suggests the greenhouse was torched. Quite a responsibility," Tim repeated.

"He's up to it." Lorna stretched, and Anna watched a gold bracelet slide down one of her slender brown arms as she

18

raised them in a vee above her head, noting without trying to that her future mother-in-law's chin line was still sharp and the only signs of age were the striations down the skin of her bare upper arms as she dropped her hands back into her lap. And there was nothing in her appearance, Anna continued to observe approvingly, to indicate effort or disguise: Lorna had slapped suncream on her face as well as her limbs after settling into her deck-chair, and her dark hair was streaked with silver.

"Let's talk about you two, now," she continued, still relaxed but showing Tim in some long-recognised subliminal way that she would not talk any more about Simon Shaw. "I'm sorry you're not being married in church, but at least you've chosen a place which used to be one before it became a concert hall, so there will be, well . . ."

"An odour of sanctity?"

"If you have to put it that way."

"And why's that a good thing, Mother? Neither of us is religious in any orthodox sense."

"I know *you're* not." Lorna turned to Anna, and assumed an exaggerated look of regret as Anna shrugged and gave her a rueful smile. "All right, but it's – well . . ."

"It's a subject you've never really thought about." Tim knew that throughout her unconventional life, while not attending church except for weddings and funerals, his mother had continued to hold 'religion' in reflex regard, in a triumvirate with the Royal Family and what had once been known as the Establishment. He even remembered her telling him, on one of her early breathless visits, to model himself on what she said rather than on what she did.

"I'm not going to argue." How often had he heard those words of retreat from a potential debate for which she had

19

no ammunition! Yet when her feelings or her mind were engaged she could present a case with fluency and skill. "At least you haven't chosen the Greffe, which would be really too clinical, just like an English register office. And as St James *was* a church and so has the space, you'll have been able to invite all the people you'd have invited to the Town church." Where Lorna herself had been married, before a large congregation; some of the black and white photographs of an uncharacteristically demure-looking woman in white beside a tall new husband showed the church in the background.

"Yes, but there aren't all that many." Tim gave an involuntary shudder as he thought of Constance Lorimer. Not as a wedding guest, of course, but inside the deconsecrated church of St James the Less a mere door's width away from his mother while he and Anna were being married. There'd be nothing to prevent it.

"And Constance Lorimer would hardly have the nerve actually to enter the Town church," Lorna said, watching him. "Whereas at St James . . ."

"There'll be people on the door there, too."

"Other things beside weddings go on in St James, darling. Art exhibitions, and so on. She'll be able to get into the building, and maybe . . ."

"Maybe into the body of the kirk to cry just impediment? There isn't any, Mother. And she has no quarrel with me. If she smoulders in the lobby so be it. And I can't believe she will. You always said she had no spirit."

"That didn't stop her trying to run me down in her car though, did it? Yes!" Anna cried out her shocked surprise. "One dark night just before Geoffrey and I escaped. I was able to get out of the way, but it was horrible. And so unnecessary – even before I appeared it was a sham of a marriage." Lorna yawned and stretched again, looking now at Tim. "I'm not concerned for myself for once, darling, I'm thinking about you and Anna. I don't want to be responsible for spoiling your perfect day."

"You won't be." But Anna, too, in the warm sunshine, experienced a *frisson* of fear. "We're both so pleased you've come, Lorna. Simon's welcome at the ceremony and at the feast," she went on, not looking at Tim because they had already reached a consensus, "if he'd like to come."

"Oh, he would!" Lorna's response was so confident Tim felt another pang of puzzled unease.

"That's fine, then," he responded heartily.

"It's kind of you both." His mother, now, sounded uncharacteristically humble. "He'll creep in at the back, of course. And mingle with the crowd afterwards."

"The top table's very short," Tim said. "Only you and Anna and me and my Sergeant Mahy as best man plus his wife, and Clare and Robin Jameson, Anna's special friends."

"No bridesmaids or matron of honour?"

"My friend Jane would have been both," Anna said regretfully, "but she lives in Cornwall and her husband's ill. I'll have Clare, though. Not behind me with a bunch of flowers, I'm not having any attendants, but she'll help me dress."

"In white?" Lorna enquired warily.

Anna laughed. "Off-white, actually. Which I suppose our grandparents would have considered totally appropriate. Not a bridal gown, Lorna, a very simple suit. And after much heart-searching, nothing on my head."

"I've a beautiful hat," Lorna told them wistfully.

"Then wear it," Anna ordered. "I'd like some glamour, and I can't think that anyone else will supply it, apart from Clare in her gorgeous outsized way. I mean that, Lorna."

21

"I can see you do," Lorna purred. "And that you're very well organised. I'm glad about that, Anna. Not having met you, I was afraid of finding myself forced to step in here, there or everywhere, but now I'm looking forward to being deliciously passive."

Anna thought that Lorna, too, meant what she was saying, but she was also aware of a sub-text for which she was grateful: that her future mother-in-law didn't see herself as being owed anything from her son's wedding beyond the unearned status of chief guest. Which she was going to enjoy.

"Two witnesses are essential in Guernsey," Lorna said. "I remember that. Who are yours, darlings?"

"Clare," Tim said, "and my sergeant Ted Mahy. There didn't seem to be any merit in widening the functional circle. And the Registrar-General will preside."

"I don't know any of the important people on the island now," Lorna said, wistful again. "Is tonight your stag night?"

"I had that a couple of nights ago. I didn't want to feel less than a hundred per cent tomorrow." Tim held his hand out sideways and Anna took it. "So nothing special tonight."

"D'you want to join Simon and me at the hotel?"

"No, he doesn't," Anna said. "But *I* should like to. I've decided to stay at the hotel tonight, Lorna, and get dressed up there in the morning. I think Tim should have a last night of bachelordom and I don't want him around while I'm getting ready."

Lorna beamed. "I was all set to persuade you to sleep in the empty bed in my room." Anna was touched to feel the sudden relaxation of Tim's hand. "But you'll be better in your own. Your last night of independence too, Anna."

Lorna was watching her closely, and Anna suspected that if she had had any lingering doubts about tying herself legally to

Tim his mother would have seen them. But there were none, and as she smiled her reassurance Anna was aware of the relief in Lorna's eyes. "I don't need it. But I don't need him within viewing distance while I'm turning myself into a bride." Anna's hesitation was brief. "You're as welcome as Clare will be, Lorna, to join me for the final stages."

"Thank you. I will. Where will you both be sleeping on Saturday night?"

"Here," Tim said. "Then the earliest plane to Glasgow on Sunday morning. We pick up our hire car at the airport there, then disappear north for a week. Will you be off on Sunday, too?" His hand clenched round Anna's.

"Oh, I think I'll wait for Simon." Lorna, now, wasn't quite meeting his eye. "He should have completed his business by Wednesday evening – he's wanting to be back in the office on Friday – so I'll take the opportunity of a few nostalgic days."

This would make for the longest stay his mother had had in Guernsey since she had ceased to live there, and that she should choose to have it during his absence evoked in Tim a disagreeable dual sensation of jealousy and anger.

Lorna was aware of it. "I'm sorry you won't be here, darling. I'll come for a week soon when you are, I promise. And I'll stay in Rouge Rue then, if you'll have me."

"Of course we will!" It was Anna who responded, but Tim was mollified enough to make the gesture he had seen for several days that he ought to make. "Look, Mother." He disengaged his hand from Anna's and leaned forward. "If you'd like to stay here while we're away you know the house is yours."

But not Simon Shaw's, Tim finished silently.

Lorna didn't hesitate. "Thank you, darling, I appreciate that absolutely enormously. But I think I'll stay on at the hotel. I feel like a few days' pampering, and I certainly don't feel like buying my meals in a supermarket. You'll have made arrangements for Duffy and the cat?"

"Of course." Tim was ashamed of his sense of relief. "Duffy's going to Clare and Robin, and my WPC Falla, who's a fanatical aleurophile, is going to feed Whitby *in situ* – she's done it before. He prefers home ground and he's learned over nearly ten years that I always come back."

"That's fine, then, darling."

"As you say, that's fine."

Anna smiled to herself as both mother and son leaned back in their chairs, having safely negotiated some nearby quicksands.

Bernard and Marjorie Charters, their son Benjamin standing between them, surveyed for the umpteenth time the charred ruins of the greenhouse which had contained what for the past five years, until the shattering suggestion made by a dinner guest, they had seen as their financial safety net. Neither Bernard nor Marjorie had ever liked the fifteenth-century Florentine religious paintings, companion pieces, which had been left to them by Bernard's brother following his death at his home in Tuscany. They had hung them in the house at first, reluctantly because they had dominated all the other artefacts in the room as well as not being to Bernard's or Marjorie's preferred taste. They had come with papers of authentication, and so Bernard had been confident in his decision, after those five uneasy years in their company, to offer them for sale. Two thefts of important art had taken place in Guernsey at the time he was making up his mind to part with the pictures, and so he had relegated them to the warm dry cupboard in the non-working greenhouse with a clear conscience.

He and Marjorie and Benjamin had been sitting in that greenhouse, as they so often did on spring and summer evenings, when their confidence was shattered by the man they were entertaining, their unofficial art expert friend Henry Thomas. They had dined in the greenhouse, and over coffee afterwards Bernard had told Henry that the pictures were to be sold, and had been so shaken by his response that he remembered every word of the conversation, every detail of the appearance of the greenhouse that warm, sunny evening: the fresh green spirals of the young-leaved plants smothering up each slim supporting column, burgeoning here and there with colour-slashed buds, the sound through the open windows of sparrows quarrelling, Marjorie's face behind a diagonal of sunlight as Henry's comment sank in.

"Oh," Henry had said, leaning back heavily in his chair, and Bernard remembered, too, the look of mild dismay on his florid face.

"What's the matter?" Marjorie had asked. Sharply.

"I'm sorry." Henry had leaned forward again. "I didn't say anything when you first showed me the pictures, because I didn't think you had any idea of selling them and I could see how happy you were just to believe in their value. Bernard, Marjorie" – Henry had held out his hands as if begging a favour – "I believe they have very little. I believe they are nineteenth-century fakes."

"No!" Marjorie had cried out, choking on the mint she was eating, and Bernard could still see the shock then in Benjamin's face, the way he had looked at his mother: protectively, then angrily at Henry. Before Marjorie's obvious distress Benjamin, Bernard recalled as he stood with his wife and son beside

25

the devastation, had had no apparent reaction to Henry's revelation. Perhaps that would have been the case with other twelve-year-olds, but Bernard was inclined, reluctantly, to put it down to the fact that Benjamin was not quite a typical boy of his age. Not backward, that wasn't the right description of his son and it wasn't one that any doctor had ever used except to say that it wasn't applicable, but – well, ever so slightly withdrawn, never in a peer group, never with a best friend, but apparently living contentedly with his own company and his own rich imagination. Benjamin *had* had a best friend, an invisible one called Cobo after the Guernsey bay they had taken him to on holiday when they still lived in England and he was beginning to talk, and the boy had been almost ten before, to Bernard and Marjorie's relief, Cobo had deserted him. But to their disappointment he hadn't put a flesh and blood friend in Cobo's place, although he seemed to get on all right at school. Bernard and Marjorie had been afraid, particularly as he approached his teens, that he might come in for some bullying because of people, young and old, tending to want to storm a citadel which has no wish to offer them admission, and had asked the headmaster to keep a watchful eye. And they were incomers to the island. Bernard and Marjorie themselves had been aware of some reserve when they had bought the land and the greenhouses and started the business, and it had taken a while to build up a clientele. But now they were accepted, and all seemed to be well for Benjamin too, in school. But although he was of course grateful for this, Bernard couldn't get rid of an uneasy feeling that Benjamin's immunity might stem from an awareness in his peers that he was somehow different from themselves. This was such a disturbing feeling, and one so difficult to put into words, he had been unable to discuss it with Marjorie. And as she had said nothing to him, he didn't know what her feelings were. Except that she had been as relieved as he was when the doctor dismissed the possibility of autism. Autistic children didn't respond to what went on around them, the doctor had told them, even by their nearest and dearest. And Benjamin did . . .

"All right, Daddy?"

As if in illustration of his thoughts, Benjamin responded now to Bernard's involuntary shiver.

"All right, son."

"No you're not, Daddy." Benjamin was starting to cry.

"Oh, darling!"

His mother took him in her arms, and the three of them turned away from the devastation and started to walk slowly back to the house. Both husband and wife were reserved by nature, even with one another, and when they were in the kitchen and Bernard turned to look at Marjorie he was shocked to see the suffering in her face.

He took her hand as she released Benjamin. "It'll be all right," he said.

She stared at him, her face now expressionless. "You think so? Insurance people are very thorough. Even if we don't tell them the pictures may not have been the real thing, somebody else will, because they'll question our business contacts. And probably our friends."

"*That* thorough?"

"We've got to be prepared for it." Marjorie looked down at her son's face, staring up at her in terror, and now Bernard saw unfamiliar compassion in her eyes. "It's all right, darling," she said softly, stroking his brow. "Go to bed."

They stood in silence as the boy went obediently from the room. When they could hear his feet on the stairs they turned and gripped each other's arms.

"Perhaps we should tell them ourselves," Marjorie whispered, "what Henry said about the pictures. Then tell them he's an amateur and that the fire happened before we'd taken them to a professional."

"If we could produce the authentication we wouldn't need to." It had been lost with the pictures, in its plastic pocket stuck to the back of one of them.

"We can get another copy."

"Where from? Your brother was a recluse."

"There must be some way. The insurance people will have the best resources. And they'll use them."

"And if they don't get anywhere?"

"Let's not think about that. And we're looking at the worst scenario. They haven't rejected our claim yet."

"Or accused us of fraud."

He looked with concern into her frantic face. "Don't even think of it. Come here."

She went obediently between his arms, but her face, hidden from his gaze as it rested on his shoulder, was expressive again of her terror of what might be to come.

Three

In the excitement of arriving at St James and waiting for Anna to join him Tim forgot about Constance Lorimer. And on his way into the one-time church whose unique round tower had been his lifetime landmark he saw only people he was comfortable with, plus a great many strangers: half the population of the island seemed to be massing in the narrow gateway on the steep hill, and a uniformed constable was on old-fashioned point duty in the road when he and Ted Mahy were driven up. Fortunately the good weather was holding, and the constable was cheerful in shirt sleeves.

"Nice, sir." Ted nodded towards the people parting willingly to either side of their car as it squeezed on to the tiny forecourt.

"It's amazing." They were all smiling, it seemed, and waving to him, which could have been another reason why he didn't think of Constance. As he got out of the car he thought about his mother's hope for the ritual, at least, of a church wedding: he and Ted arriving first and sitting front right of the centre aisle, Anna walking up it to meet them as they moved out to stand beside her. He had conceded his and Ted's prior arrival, but was happy with Anna's preference for travelling with his mother and the Jamesons and joining him and Ted in the foyer so that they would enter the hall together and make their way as a group up the aisle and on to the hallowed ground of the platform where over the years so many musicians had entertained him. Anna had at first recoiled from the idea of being married on a stage, but had reluctantly agreed when Tim pointed out that if they were elevated there would be no craning of necks among the congregation and all their friends would be true witnesses. And after one consultation she had been happy to leave the choice and arrangement of the flowers, on the stage and off it, to Clare, whose exuberantly unique floral decoration of the greenhouses flanking her nursing home Anna always enjoyed.

Tim had been part of St James stage marriages before, both as best man and witness, and realised with an inward smile as he climbed the central steps, flanked this time by huge bowls of pink-tinged white flowers among which he fleetingly recognised marguerites and roses, that during each of them he had been profoundly thankful not to be the groom. As he gained the platform now he tried to test himself for any doubts that this time it was his right role, but the idea of not marrying Anna was so impossible he abandoned the test as soon as he had set it in favour of gazing with loving approval on his bride, not turned into an alien, fairy-tale creature by a long white gown and a veil but still, even in the simple skirt and jacket and classic blue silk blouse, someone at that moment mysterious, far away in the instant of presenting herself to become legally part of him.

A glorious paradox! Tim found himself grinning at her in his sudden elation, and was happy that her mystery disappeared as she grinned back.

Anna, too, had attempted a test, tried to think of herself as a drowning woman recalling the wonders of independence, and had abandoned the exercise as irrelevant. But was Tim as sure? she wondered in an uncharacteristic moment of panic which showed her as it shocked her how necessary he had become to her. And then he grinned at her, and she was restored to her quietly confident self.

The Registrar-General, coming round from behind the table on which were the documents to be signed and a vase of red roses Clare had insisted on picking from her own garden, welcomed the wedding party and then the twenty or so rows of wedding guests and reminded all present of the solemn and binding nature of the short ceremony about to take place.

That was the moment, joining the Registrar-General in his survey of the witnesses, that Tim remembered Constance Lorimer. It took a savage effort of will, aided by his knowledge that he had ordered two members of the force to be stationed the far side of the hall doors, to forget her. But he was pleased to see that Simon Shaw was one of just six people in the last occupied row to the right of the aisle. *Friend of the bridegroom.* Only he didn't know him . . .

The introduction was over, the Registrar-General was addressing him personally and he must respond in the words being put into his mouth. Words he knew by heart.

"I do solemnly declare that I know not of any lawful impediment why I, Timothy James Le Page, may not be joined in matrimony to Anna Elizabeth Weston."

A benign silence, in which he turned towards Anna. She had already turned towards him, and he spoke again.

"I call upon the persons here present to witness that I, Timothy James Le Page, do take thee, Anna Elizabeth Weston, to be my lawful wedded wife . . ." *Pour être ma femme legalement mariée*, Tim concluded in his head. Over the years the French words had become as familiar as the English.

"I call upon the persons here present," Anna responded in her usual quiet clear voice, "to witness that I, Anna Elizabeth

Weston, do take thee, Timothy James Le Page, to be my lawful wedded husband."

Then the Registrar-General was nodding to Ted, who handed him the gold bands, one of which the Registrar-General handed to Tim. Tim, feeling the ring warm and slightly damp from its sojourn in Ted's palm, eased it onto Anna's thin finger, realising as he did so that he had never until that moment seen a ring on her marriage finger, not even a circle of pale skin where one might have been worn the previous summer . . . The ring Anna was sliding on to his finger was warm, too.

The Registrar-General, his smile widening to a beam, was pronouncing them man and wife, authorising the bridegroom to kiss the bride – Tim obeyed with a butterfly brush he knew was the most Anna would want in public – and then they were being invited over to the table, to turn what they had said into law. Straightening up from writing his name in the indicated places, Tim for the second time looked out over the congregation and saw his mother, her eyes glittering, lean into the aisle and look back along it at the moment Simon Shaw made a similar move. There was no doubt that they exchanged glances, and Anna looked at him sharply as his left hand, clasping hers, involuntarily clenched.

"All right, Tim?"

"Of course. I just saw – Mother and Shaw."

"So did I. But we're married, Tim."

"I know, I know. It's all that matters."

When they had reached the outer doors, and were halted by the photographer, the first person Tim saw was Constance Lorimer. Just to the inside of the gates, standing against the railings with her friend Beth Smith. He'd forgotten about Beth Smith, so self-effacing and quietly spoken, but remembered now her frequent presence at Constance's side following the disappearance from the island of Constance's husband with Lorna . . .

The photographer was beckoning them forward into the sunshine, beckoning Ted and Lorna and Clare and Robin to stand either side of them, and Constance Lorimer's blank face was suddenly alive with rage. Beth Smith's was tense and strained as she held Constance back by the arm when she started to move forward, and Constance, thank heaven, was obeying, was retreating to the wall, where both women stood wide-eyed, chests heaving. As the photographer paused between shots Tim glanced across at his mother.

She too was aware of Constance, he could see it in the elaborately nonchalant way she was staring through the two women by the railings, half smiling. Constance saw it too, and reacted with a fist clenched shoulder-high and a distortion of the mouth as if she was shouting abuse. But if she was, it was drowned in the cheers and shouts of goodwill from the rest of the waiting crowd. Anna was half smiling at everyone; she had never knowingly seen Constance Lorimer, and Tim was glad she was unaware of the mimed drama. Which his mother seemed to be enjoying, he realised with the familiar dual reaction of amusement and exasperation.

"You'll come with us!" he ordered her, when the first car squeezed in as the photographer released them.

"But I'm going with the Jamesons and your sergeant! You and Anna have to travel on your own!"

"No, we don't, Mother. But get in the front if it worries you. Constance Lorimer worries *me*."

"*That* poor soul!" Lorna hissed contemptuously. But she saw the determination in her son's face and got reluctantly into the front seat of the car when Tim had signalled to the driver to unlock the passenger door, not without a concerned glance back into St James in an attempt, Tim was sure, to catch a glimpse of Simon Shaw.

But he had been learning since childhood not to let his mother upset him, and as he settled into the back of the car beside Anna the pinpricks ceased.

"All right?" she asked him again.

"Oh, yes." They kissed less decorously.

"Tim," Anna said, as she drew away, "you saw Constance Lorimer, didn't you? Were you afraid your mother might tackle her?"

"I was afraid she might tackle my mother, the way she was looking. At least, that she might come up to her while she and Ted and the Jamesons were waiting for the second car. Getting her away quickly seemed like a sensible safety measure."

"I hope she won't follow us to the Duke."

"Let's not think about it, we don't want Constance Lorimer to be part of our memories of today." *Nor Simon Shaw*, Tim added in his head. But at least there was no danger of Simon making a scene. Getting himself into a press photograph . . . He wasn't going to let either Simon or Constance Lorimer spoil his wedding day.

Nevertheless he hustled his mother up the hotel steps.

"You both look fine to me," he said in the foyer, surveying her and Anna judicially. "But if you feel you need to repair anything . . . I'm told the ladies' room here is a home from home. Unless you'd rather go upstairs."

"The ladies' room," Anna said, looking at Lorna.

"But the bride . . ." Lorna protested. "Other people – guests – might come in while we're there, and the bride—"

"I'm no mystical bride figure," Anna assured her, "and I shan't worry if they do. Which they may not if we're quick." She took Lorna's hand. "Come on! Back in a minute, Tim."

If Lorna had been a woman carefully preserved physically, Anna reflected as they sped away, whose elegance depended on props and cosmetics, she would have given her the choice of where to retire to, but having observed her mother-in-law (the thought of Lorna Le Page being her mother-in-law was far stranger than the thought of Tim being her husband) she was confident she would need only to take stock of her hat and hair and renew her lipstick. In the event Lorna removed her hat, a gorgeous and becoming complex of light straw, and gave it over to the cloakroom attendant, reviving her hair with her hands.

"A hat can inhibit movement of the jaws," she observed to Anna's mirrored image. "Have you noticed? I'm hungry and I'm looking forward to the food. You know, Anna" – her gaze was suddenly serious and thoughtful – "you've got what I've got. Flair. You know by instinct what suits you. It's worth buckets of cosmetics."

"Thank you. I don't bother much, really." But Anna was pleased. "We'd better go," she said. "We're not intending to form a reception line, but I think we should be first into the restaurant."

In effect they were a group at the door, so that Anna and Tim could be sure of presenting all their friends and partners to Lorna. To Tim's annoyance, he found himself scanning the influx of guests for the presence of Constance Lorimer; he had warned Reception to be ready for a dressed-down, middle-aged woman with a wild air to her, but knew even as he was alerting the politely attentive young man and young woman behind the counter how unlikely it was they would be able to pick Constance out of the throng of guests, or summon the confidence to detain a woman who answered his imprecise description . . .

"Anna! Tim! How splendid!" The booming voice of Anne's boss Brian Bradshaw surmounted the quiet hubbub. Brian had the looks to go with his voice, Anna thought, as the tall broad figure with the shock of black hair and thick black brows enveloped her in a bear hug.

"I'm glad, Anna. Be happy." Brian's wife Laura, elegant by artifice and seen generally as a sourpuss, but Anna had somehow breached her defences, even persuaded her to get a job at the Guille-Allès library in town and make use of her librarian qualifications. But Laura, of course, regarded Lorna with suspicion; most people still, despite her Anna-induced concessions, were guilty in her eyes until proved innocent.

"Anna dear, I'm so happy for you." John Coquelin, soft-spoken second in command at the surgery, always civil and contained. Anna didn't know how far John had recovered from the trauma of his girlfriend's violent death and suspected that no one else did, either.

"Oh, Anna! Lovely, lovely!" Joy Smith, the vet practice assistant and dogsbody, remembered Anna's reserve halfway through an exuberant embrace, and stepped hastily back.

"Thank you, Joy." Anna retained the girl's hand for a moment, to show her she had appreciated Joy's spontaneity. Joy's boyfriend Cliff Ozanne, the fourth vet in the practice, shook hands with Anna as formally as with Tim, ever wary since admitting in an uncontrolled and regretted moment that he had hoped for the junior partnership. Wary again, as he glanced over his shoulder at Pam Francis, close behind him and an attractive local girl who had recently taken over Reception. Anna noticed Joy glancing back, too, with a frown. Cliff was being noticeably less taciturn with Pam than he was with most people, and if the new girl hadn't been so obviously

uninterested in him Anna would have been braced for a drama
in their midst.

Nicky Torode, Tim's newish DC, possibly the most glamorous of the young female guests but still looking fearsomely
efficient, which Tim had told Anna she was. Nicky made Anna
consciously grateful, for a moment, that she had total faith in
her husband's loyalty.

A bunch of Tim's young colleagues, a couple of them a bit
teasing, but all showing Anna that they liked and respected
him. Lorna was flirtatious with them as a group, which they
obviously enjoyed, and Anna was amused to see one of them
look with surprise from her to her son. Alerted by Tim's
muttered identification, Lorna greeted her son's Chief and his
wife with dignified graciousness.

Simon Shaw was almost the last. Anna glanced at the two
politely blank faces as he and Tim shook hands, then found
herself smiling at the boy as she held hers out. "I hope you'll
be very happy," Simon said quietly. He hadn't said anything
to Tim.

"Thank you. If I don't get a chance to speak to you again,
I hope you enjoy your stay in Guernsey as well as getting your
business done."

"Thank you." The boy gave her a long, grave look and then,
with a little bow, moved on to Lorna. Without turning fully
towards them Anna was aware that he had bent to kiss her,
and heard the murmur of their voices.

Both Tim and Anna, and each of them with annoyance, felt
a sense of relief when the half-hour of standing around with
glasses was ended by the voice of the hotel proprietor and it
became possible to see precisely who was in the restaurant. A
friend of both Tim and Anna and, with his wife, just back like
everyone else in his restaurant from St James, he led them and

their small party to the top table, before suggesting to the guests that they colonise the smaller round tables and then attack the display of food, as wide and colourful as a herbaceous border, that stretched across the opposite wall.

"We're the élite, we're being waited on!" Lorna had spotted the shyness of DS Mahy's small, stout wife, hanging back with a nervous smile and her handbag in a twitchy grip, and was taking her by the hand as Tim and Ted came up. "I'm Lorna, Tim's mother. I know you're Mrs Ted, but I don't know your own name."

"It's Marilyn." Dazzled by Lorna's radiant smile and attentive presence, Marilyn Mahy blinked.

"Marilyn can sit beside me, can't she, Tim?" Lorna asked. "So long as you and Anna are at the centre and I'm next to her and Ted next to you . . . Oh, dear, that means you'll have to choose between me and your husband as a neighbour, Marilyn."

"Oh, dear . . . I don't . . ." Mrs Mahy's face flamed red. Not for the first time, Tim noted resignedly, the teasing element in his mother's make-up had clashed with the compassionate, and the object of her compassion had been disturbed rather than reassured. But Lorna moved in an aura of unexpectness, and Tim wasn't really surprised when, suddenly positive, Mrs Mahy elected to sit next to Mr Le Page's mother.

Clare sent her handsome husband to the end of the top table on Mrs Mahy's side and settled down to an animated chat about flower arranging with the wife of the Duke's proprietor, who had wreathed the restaurant in white and gold and, reluctantly agreeing to let her husband preside on his own, sat down next to Clare, enabling the bride and bridegroom, to the expressed satisfaction of the photographer, to be the precise centre of the line.

At least, Tim thought, as a colourful plate of food was put before him, he wouldn't have to sit through a eulogy of his bride from a father or a father figure, mentally adjusting his own sketchily prepared speech to accommodate appreciation of its wit and comment on the revelations it had offered. No one had given away that free spirit Anna Weston, and he need thank no one before thanking the guests for their gifts and their presence, and the hotel for its catering and its flowers. Ted would be spared entirely, as there were no bridesmaids. Within minutes of their cutting the elegant small cake the hotel had made for them, another of his friends, the Duke's resident musician, would be slipping behind the curtain into the ballroom, where he would join his small team and strike up the band.

Simon Shaw was sitting with his Chief, Tim noticed with another small shock, and in fluent conversation. He couldn't see the restaurant doors from his place at the top table, but waiters were milling in front of it, and Constance Lorimer certainly wasn't in the room . . .

"Are you hungry?" he asked Anna. "I'm not, at all. Which is odd, as everything looks so good."

"I know, but I'm not hungry either." Both glanced at Lorna, putting her knife and fork together on an empty plate, then smiled at one another. But Lorna as she looked up found Simon's eye, and the smile that passed between them put paid to Tim's.

Anna took his hand under the table. "You can't do anything about it, and friends can be close, and concerned about one another, without . . . Here comes the cake."

Hand over hand they made the incision, and when the cake had been carried off for cutting up Anna sat down and Tim stayed on his feet, a piece of card in his hand that he didn't look at. "Family." With an affectionate glance at his mother. "Friends." His glance toured the room. "Thank you for being with my wife and me today." His historic speech was under way and Anna was able to relax and enjoy it, confident from the times she had already heard him address groups of people that he would enjoy it too, although today he had no knowledge to impart, he had only what he himself jokily called wedding and after-dinner speeches – 'a few well-chosen words'.

Anna came to attention with a shiver of excitement, as she realised she was going to learn something new about her husband: the extent of his public wit. And that if he turned out to have little or none she wouldn't care. How she had changed! In her past relationships her mind had always been in the ascendant over her heart, assessing would-be partners for their intelligence above and beyond their other qualities. Except with Jimmy. Not that Jimmy wasn't intelligent – although it didn't much show on his surface – but that wasn't why she had married him. She hadn't married Tim for his mind, either, any more than for his body, she had married him because he was Tim, for better or worse. And his short speech was proving to be for better. Anna thought – and hoped – that her relief at discovering this was for him rather than for herself.

He had turned to Ted. "Bit of a cushy number, you might think, being best man at a wedding where there are no bridesmaids to do the gallant thing by. But I can assure you all that Ted Mahy has done a vital job in helping me to reach today in one piece – in a whole range of ways he would hate me to detail – as well as being a steady presence at my side. So let us turn precedent on its head and drink to – the best man!"

Typical Tim to sit down with his audience's attention

directed away from himself, Anna reflected as she raised her glass. But now Ted had been given his opportunity he quickly directed the spotlight back on to the bridal couple with a few words ending in a toast, before slipping out on Tim's signal to alert the musicians.

That was when people began to leave their seats and move around, and at the first notes of music some of them began to go through to the ballroom. Tim and Anna joined them promptly, on the shared thought that a small audience for their opening dance would be preferable to a large one. They had taken only a few applauded turns before Tim indicated to Ted to join them with Marilyn, and soon Lorna was on the floor with Simon. Decorously, Anna noted, alerted to their presence by the brief rigidity of Tim's arms. She and Tim must dance together again, she thought, the experience was bringing back the excitement of newness, making her feel, absurdly, that their first married night would be their first night together.

"I'm enjoying this," Tim whispered. "But I think you'd better be available for a while to other men."

The first of the other men was Simon Shaw. "Thank you for inviting me today," he said. He was a good dancer, too, and similar to Tim in height and build. "I do so hope you and Tim are going to have a wonderful life."

"We expect to." His eyes were large and blue, his skin creamy brown, his hair golden. Anna noted with amusement that several of the younger female guests were aware of him. Also Lorna, who to Anna's relief was smiling on them approvingly.

"I hope I'll be able to feel like that with somebody one day." A sentiment to cheer Tim when she reported it? He could hardly be speaking of Lorna. "Anna" – Simon's face

41

now was diffident – "I have an idea that Lorna . . . Did she tell you and Tim what I'm doing here?"

"She did." Anna's rueful smile was met by an indulgent one, but Simon's face immediately clouded.

"Did Tim . . . ? What did he think of my profession?"

Why should he think anything of it? Tim would have had the same reaction. But she had to reassure Simon's ridiculous anxiety.

"He was intrigued. He doesn't think that everyone should be part of the Establishment. We both hope you'll be successful."

Looking out over the dance floor a little later, Anna saw that Simon was dancing with one of the prettiest girls. And that Lorna's face as she regarded them was still serene.

Four

O nly one member of each workforce – Ted Mahy and John Coquelin – knew that the bride and bridegroom were going back to Rouge Rue for their first married night. Neither Tim nor Anna was seriously worried about more people finding out, but neither relished the thought of a jokey siege of the villa and both were attracted by the idea of the slight ingenuity needed to outwit their friends and their other colleagues.

So they had not said when or where they were going for their honeymoon, nor contradicted the expressed assumption that they would be catching the last plane of the day to London. Ted had let himself be seen to disappear towards the end of the celebrations and to return some twenty minutes later in a private hire car, the boot of which he took care to indicate contained holiday luggage.

"They're well organised," Marilyn Mahy, who was not in the secret, whispered to Lorna, who was.

"Yes. People can behave so oddly at these times, they thought it would be wise. As it is they'll be tailed to the airport, you'll see."

Lorna went with them in the car, and as a special favour was allowed through with them into the departure lounge. It was a special favour for Tim and Anna to be allowed through, too, as they were leaving not by plane but in John Coquelin's car, waiting for them outside an obscure door allocated for their escape.

"When I went back into the lobby," Lorna told them triumphantly on the telephone a half-hour later, "there was quite a crowd. Some of them even hung on to watch the London plane take off. Were there any clever clogs by John's car?"

"None. And no one at the gate when we got home. Mission successfully accomplished, and with no one left feeling frustrated – by the time we're back and it leaks out, it'll be history." Tim hesitated. "Have you . . . Did you see Constance Lorimer again?"

"No! She's made her gesture, darling."

"I hope you're right. Are you off to bed now?" Anna saw Tim's knuckles whiten as he strengthened his grip on the telephone.

"After we've walked to the lookout and surveyed the lights and the other islands. It's a lovely night."

"You and Simon?" Tim wished immediately that he hadn't asked the question. But it had been reflex.

"Me and Simon. Have a wonderful week, both of you. I'll come back soon to see you."

"We both hope you will. I'm glad you've been with us today, Mother. There'd have been a gap if you hadn't come."

He heard the long, contented sigh. "I *do* get much more than I deserve, don't I? Thank you, darling."

"Take care. Look," Tim went on quickly, because he had to, "I really mean that. Constance Lorimer knows where you're staying."

"I told you, darling, she's done her worst. Made it clear she's neither forgotten nor forgiven. But it's in the past. Geoffrey's dead, rest his soul. And . . ." Tim heard the sharp sudden breath.

"Yes?"

"That's it, isn't it? Don't go on, Tim."

It was an order. "All right, it's only that I'm concerned about you."

"I know, darling, and it's the wonder of my life. Goodnight and God bless."

Anna took Tim's hand as he put the telephone down, looking round the cosy, unfashionable sitting-room with its high Victorian mantelpiece, crowded, as were the two display cabinets, with the pieces of porcelain and the curios no one else in Tim's family had wanted. "Do you remember that first time you brought me here? How formal we were, and then . . ."

"Because we were aching for one another and could neither of us imagine that the other was feeling the same." He pulled her arm up round his neck. "We can't fall over Duffy on the stairs tonight and the cat seems out for the count." He nodded towards the fireside chair in which Whitby was a tight grey circle. "So?"

"Oh, yes! When we were dancing . . ."

They raced upstairs, tore off their clothes. An hour or so later, when they had just drifted into sleep, the telephone rang.

"Has to be a wrong number," Tim mumbled crossly. "Nobody knows we're here."

"The people who matter do. You'd better answer it."

"God, yes!" He was bolt upright, his teeth chattering and his hand trembling, so that the telephone clattered to the floor and he had to grope for it.

"Hello," he said at last. Not *DI Le Page*, in his usual way.

"Tim? Simon here."

"Simon?" *Why not my mother*? He had known for ever that there was something terribly wrong.

"Tim, Lorna's in hospital. But she's *all right*. She's all right, Tim."

"Constance Lorimer." Another reflex, making him realise how uneasy the woman had made him.

"Hit-and-run. So I suppose it could have been."

So his mother had told Shaw about Constance. "But *you're* all right. You let her walk closer to the road." He regretted that as soon as he'd said it. But he was so fearfully angry. "I'm sorry," he muttered.

"We'd only just come down the hotel steps." Shaw's voice was without expression, as if he had not heard Tim's terrible accusation. "One of her earrings flew off, we watched it land in the road and she ran after it. She couldn't see it or get hold of it right away. While she was scrabbling she asked me to look for the bit that goes behind the ear, which she said should be on the pavement, and I was doing that when I heard the car and then saw it tearing up from the lookout towards Cambridge Park Road. It was so quick, Tim. Lorna slipped trying to get to her feet. I hurled myself into the road and caught hold of her by one shoulder as the car hit the other. Or something like that. It didn't go over her, it just knocked us both backwards. At least she ended up on me and not on the road. Her left shoulder's dislocated and her left leg's badly cut, but otherwise she's okay."

"What about you?" Tim had to force himself not to sound grudging.

"A few bruises. I'm all right."

"Good. Did you get the car number?"

"I'm afraid not. I was Lorna's cushion and by the time we'd sorted ourselves out the car was well away. And when it was coming at her . . . well, it was her I was looking at."

"It *was* coming at her?"

"I'd say so. The driver had to have seen her but he or she wasn't slowing down, they were accelerating. I think it was

46

dark – the car, I mean – and not very large, but that's all I can tell you. She's comfortable here in the Princess Elizabeth, she's asleep in fact, and I'll be going back to the hotel when – when I've been given the once-over."

Tim wondered if Shaw was playing his own injuries up by playing them down. Wondered, on a flash of surreal horror, if he had been in cahoots with the driver of the car, manoeuvring Lorna into the road . . .

"I'll be over right away. Maybe see you."

"Right . . . Tim, I'm sorry. Your wedding night . . ."

"That's of no practical significance, as I'm sure you know. Where do I go?"

"Victoria wing."

"I'll be there in twenty minutes."

There wasn't much he had to fill in for Anna.

"You'll be going as a policeman as well as a next of kin, won't you?"

"I suppose I will." He was shocked to realise he had been thinking of himself *vis-à-vis* an attempted murder as no more than the victim's son. "I'm officially on leave but that goes by the board when . . ." He turned a horrified face to her as he snapped on the light. "Oh, God, darling. Scotland."

"I'll cancel while you're away. The plane at least. I'll wait till the morning to ring the hire car firm and the hotels."

"Oh, Anna. Once I've seen for myself Mother really is all right, perhaps we could . . ." Tim stopped, turned to look at her as he said it aloud. "But it could have been murder."

"Which means that as detective inspector you're going to *have* to be here as well as wanting to be. Tim, we had a wonderful wedding day. Get up and go."

It *was* a lovely night, Tim agreed bitterly as he opened the garage. Still, and mild, and scented. The starry sky was obscured here and there by pale puffs of cloud and a deluded robin was twittering softly, perhaps awakened by the safety light now illumining his small front garden. The only song bird, now that high summer had arrived, to be still singing. Tim had all his life been aware of the flora and fauna surrounding him, and each year lamented the morning and evening chorus as it tailed away in mid-July.

The short drive to the hospital seemed very long, and his internal walk seemed to go on for ever. The senior duty nurse in the Victoria wing told him the physical story: his mother's left shoulder had been manipulated back into place and the cuts on her leg cleaned up under the sufficient anaesthesia of a dose of morphine. The shoulder would have to be strapped up, and the leg wounds regularly dressed, for at least a week. It wasn't possible at the moment to say how long they would be keeping her in the hospital, as it was too early to assess the extent of her shock.

"No stitches in the leg, fortunately," the nurse concluded. Tim knew he would always remember the way a top tooth jutted over her lip as she offered him a reassuring smile, and the shiny yellow wall behind her of the small office in which they were standing. A uniformed constable he had last seen on the Duke of Richmond dance floor was sitting outside the room to which a junior nurse escorted him. As he spotted Tim and scrambled to his feet he registered a shocked compassion which he immediately tried to banish from his face. "Sir . . . I'm sorry, sir," he mumbled, before freezing into an impassivity worthy of a Buckingham Palace sentry.

"Thank you, Constable. You may relax." At another time the man's dilemma would have amused him. "Has my mother said anything?"

"I've not been allowed yet to speak to her." The constable cast a rueful glance at the severe-faced nurse.

"She's asleep," the nurse said, her severity softening to uncertainty as she turned to Tim and registered a mingling of reflex disapproval of a policeman about to upset a patient, and compassion for an anxious relative. That dilemma could have amused him, too. "But I suppose . . . *You* may go in," she conceded briskly, her face sharpening again into a quelling glance at the junior policeman.

"Thank you," Tim responded gratefully. "Don't go away, Constable," he said, as the nurse bustled off. "I'll probably be doing your work for you and if so you can take it down for your report."

He was as thankful as he would have been as a child to see that the lovely face was unmarked. But it was unnaturally pale and seemed to have shed flesh in the short time since he had last seen it. She was lying on her right side and her left shoulder was heavily bandaged. He thought she was asleep, but as he slid silently into the chair by the bed she opened her large dark eyes and smiled at him.

"Hello, darling." It was a sleepy whisper that immediately reassured him.

"Mother. You're all right?"

"No. I'm worried about you and Anna and Scotland." The whisper had risen to a murmur. "No need for you not to go. In fact if you don't go I shall be extremely angry."

He didn't have to force his smile. "That's very unselfish of you." And very characteristic, her egotism had always been shot through with understanding of other people. "But we don't want to leave you. And you needn't be angry, because even if we were prepared to go we couldn't. I'm the detective inspector and" – for a moment he hesitated – "from what

49

Simon has told me, what happened could have been attempted murder."

"It *was* attempted murder." Tim was glad to see that the wide eyes retained their power to flash. "She failed the first time, so she's tried again."

"Constance Lorimer kept her anger at that pitch for thirty years?"

"She didn't have to. She just had to see me again for it all to come back."

See that you're still a beautiful, desirable woman. Tim thought of how Constance Lorimer had looked that afternoon inside the railings at St James's: plain, dumpy, faded, and full of rage. Against all his training, he found himself convinced of her unproven guilt. And her unstable state of mind. No one with their sense of self-preservation intact would have attempted to kill in a way that pointed so obviously to the culprit.

"Mother, when you're able to leave hospital you'll have to go straight back to England."

"If you'll let me confront her on my way to the airport. With you as my police escort."

"We'll see. Now, do you feel up to telling me what happened?"

"Of course, darling."

It was a long time since he had opened a notebook for such a purpose. Shaw came well out of her account.

"If he hadn't grabbed me the way he did, Tim, the car would have gone over some part of me, I'm sure of it. I wonder his arms didn't come out of their sockets, he yanked me so hard. He was hurt too, you know. I made them tell me about him before I agreed to take the painkillers. I . . . ." Perhaps it was because she had seen the involuntary tightening of his face, perhaps because she realised she could be giving something away about her feeling for Simon Shaw, that Lorna tailed off. Tim suspected her yawn of being manufactured. But he got to his feet.

"You must sleep now. I'll be back in the morning. I'm glad Simon was with you." But if he hadn't been, she wouldn't have been jaunting off to the lookout in the dark.

"Say goodnight to Anna. I'm so sorry, darling. Your wedding day . . .".

She really did seem to be falling asleep. Tim kissed her, left the ward, and dictated what she had said to the grateful constable. He had just finished as Simon Shaw appeared. There was a plaster on his left cheek and his left arm was in a sling.

"Contact with the pavement," he said lightly, touching the plaster.

"And the arm?" Tim asked.

"Only bruised. Have you seen her?"

"Yes. She gave me a statement which I've passed on to the constable here, so that's done with. She's gone back to sleep."

Tim stopped speaking and they looked steadily at one another. Tim knew his eyes were telling Shaw to go away, but wasn't sure what Shaw's were saying because of the sadness in them.

"Look, she's all right." He hadn't known he was going to be reassuring. "But I'd rather you didn't disturb her now. I think you and I should have a chat, but it can wait till the morning. Can you come and see me at the station? Say eleven, give you time to rest." He knew eleven would be all right for him, he had no appointments.

He hadn't expected the man's face to brighten. "Yes, Tim! I'll be there."

"Good. Give you a lift now to the hotel? It's on my way home."

The brightness died. Shaw looked resigned, and Tim knew he had been intending to disobey him and go in to Lorna. "Thanks, that would be a help, my hire car's at the Duke."

"I realised that."

They didn't talk on the short journey to the hotel, and Shaw slipped out of Tim's car with the one word "Thanks". As he let himself into his house Tim saw a light in the kitchen. Anna was sitting in her dressing-gown at the old scrubbed wooden table, and there was steam rising from the kettle spout.

She got up as he came in and went to warm the waiting teapot, waiting herself, characteristically, for him to speak.

"She's all right," he said at once. "Still herself. The shoulder's back in place and there was no need for stitches in her leg, but they'll keep her in for a few days. She's convinced it was Constance Lorimer, although neither she nor Shaw really saw anything."

"*You* can't be convinced it was. Come and sit down." She put a mug in front of him, pressed his hand briefly as she resumed her seat on one of the two old white-painted bentwood chairs.

Tim sank on to the other one. "I know, but how can I think of the woman as innocent?"

"Perhaps whoever it was was after Simon. His sleuthing assignment?"

"He's hardly had time to start."

"He could still have blown it."

"On his first day? It was Mother in the road, so we have to begin by looking for someone who wanted to harm Mother. Constance Lorimer showed her hostility in public yesterday. Which makes it easy for me to ask her to let me have a look at her car. That's going to be my priority, after I've explained to the Chief why I've put myself back on duty. Shaw's coming to see me at the office at eleven, so he can tell me about his first day's work. Now, it's only half past two, so let's go back to bed."

"Yes. I got through to the airport and cancelled our flight." Anna looked with amusement at his bewildered face and ruffled his hair. "You'd forgotten, hadn't you? That you hadn't intended going to work today?"

"For a moment, yes. Oh, darling, I'm sorry. When Shaw rang and told me . . . It was like I'd always known and I think the idea of going away disappeared then. Are you very disappointed?"

"Of course not. We've got forever after, and I want you to catch whoever tried to kill your mother. When you leave in the morning I'll ring the hire car people and the hotels." She grinned at him as she got to her feet. "Then go back to work myself, and wonder by lunchtime how they could have managed without me."

To their surprise both of them slept, although Tim did some uninterpretable mumbled talking that disturbed Anna a couple of times. They woke finally earlier than usual, too tense for dalliance, and it wasn't quite eight o'clock when Tim reached the featureless green stretch of Cambridge Park with Duffy, and saw a pale sun rising over the curve of L'Hyvreuse where it descended towards the lookout. He also saw, to his satisfaction, a couple of constables examining the roadway outside the Duke of Richmond Hotel; he had told the constable at the hospital to contact the station and ask for an early check.

"Anything?" He let Duffy go, and the streetwise dog bounded on to the grass and began to tear round in circles.

The constables straightened up. "Nothing, sir," one of them said, and the other shook his head.

"Ah." Tim's disappointment made him realise that Constance Lorimer's dilapidated appearance the day before had made him hope at least for a bit of rust. But from what he had heard, the injuries to his mother as well as to Simon Shaw had come from the violence of their retreat as much as from the impact of the car. And a thread of nylon from Lorna's tights would be more traceable on a tyre than on a roadway. Until the driver cleaned up . . .

"Come on, Duffy!"

As always the dog bounded over to him when he heard Tim's voice, and they set off back to Rouge Rue, Tim in a sudden fever of anxiety to get to Constance Lorimer, even though his common sense told him that if she was guilty she must already have taken what action she could to obliterate any trace of impact on her car.

It was still only twenty past eight, and he forced himself to make a pot of tea and eat a piece of toast with Anna before ringing his Chief and then setting out again, this time by car, to collect an alerted and speechlessly sympathetic DS Mahy from his home down town and drive north with him along the coast road to St Sampson.

It was to be another settled day, Tim knew from the pastel start it was making, a hazy sun casting a delicate light on the grey-green sea to their right. Constance Lorimer lived at the back of the island's second town, still in the house she had shared with her husband until Lorna Le Page had taken him away. An uglier house than the attractive older stuccoed villas alongside it, although it was set back from the building line in a small surround of its own ground. As he parked on the short driveway in front of the closed garage door, Tim remembered how disdainful of the property his mother had been, and recalled its origins aloud to Ted.

"A speculative builder bought the land in the thirties and there was quite a for and against controversy in the *Press* when he built on it in the style of the moment." The flat steel bars on the curving sunshine windows looked, now, like dirty sticking plaster, and the Art Deco sunburst over the front door had lost a ray.

"It hasn't worn well."

"It hasn't been maintained." Because the deserted wife had lost heart? Tim was for the first time ashamed that under the influence of his mother he had never accorded Constance Lorimer a jot of pity.

The second sunburst was intact: an orange orb rising from a royal-blue sea in a stained-glass oval set into the top half of the front door. Tim studied it as he waited for the door to open, and had to lower his gaze to meet Constance Lorimer's deep-set, suspicious eyes.

"I'm Detective Inspector Le Page and this is—"

"I know who both of you are. What do you want?" A cigarette hung from her full lower lip, and her voice had grown deeper and more husky since Tim had last heard it.

"We want to have a look at your car, Mrs Lorimer."

No reaction beyond a deepening of the suspicion, but if she was guilty she as well as her car would be ready for him, and Tim tried to damp down his excitement. "What for?"

"Because last night someone tried to run my mother down outside the Duke of Richmond hotel." The sharp intake of breath, the sudden clenched grip on the door frame, looked like a reaction to shock, but whether real or feigned there was no way of divining. "And yesterday afternoon, following my wedding, you were seen to make threatening gestures to her outside St James."

"So that means I'd try to kill her? I don't wish her well, God knows, she destroyed my life, but even that wouldn't turn me into a murderer."

"You tried once before."

He was surprised to see the putty-coloured face blush, it had looked so bloodless. "Not to kill her, man, just to give her a shock. I didn't touch her. And it was thirty years ago."

"So perhaps you intended to give her a second shock?"

"I might have done, yes," she said judicially, still looking up boldly into his eyes. "I might have taken a run at her and her latest fancy man. Oh, yes, I could see she's still at it. But I didn't. I didn't take my car out yesterday, Mr Le Page. Neither Beth nor I was fool enough to think we could park anywhere near St James; we went by bus, and came home the same way. And I washed the car yesterday morning, so you won't find any marks on it anywhere."

"You'd be surprised, Mrs Lorimer, what forensic experts can find these days." There was a confidence in DS Mahy's voice which Tim couldn't believe he was feeling: if Constance Lorimer had dried her car properly, they were unlikely to be able to prove she had washed it twenty-four hours later than she was claiming.

"They can't find what can't be there."

"Washing a car won't remove a dent."

"Hurt that badly, was she?" For the first time Tim saw light in the eyes.

"She was hurt. Open the garage doors for us will you please, Mrs Lorimer?"

"Of course, Inspector. I'll get the key."

Constance Lorimer didn't invite them into the house but she left the front door open, and both men stood silently surveying the gloomy hall, Tim wondering if Ted too was aware of the musty smell which made him glad to be out on the step.

When Mrs Lorimer reappeared she pulled the door to, then led them the short way along the cracked concrete path under the ground floor sunshine window to the garage.

That, too, had its original facade, now heavily distressed: black double doors with crazed glass panels in their upper halves, sliding away each side in grooves. Tim's heart leaped as he saw that the car was a small black Fiesta, then sank as he saw too that it was far from new and had had more than one encounter with other objects. It was also, as Constance Lorimer had promised, washed clean. She had backed it into the garage, and it was easy to see the front nearside mudguard and panel which would have made contact with his mother, and that the small dents and scratches it carried were much the same as those on the offside.

Tim hadn't thought he was expecting anything better, but his disappointment was painful. It was a welcome distraction to see the pick-up truck at the gate, arrived to time.

After a glance at Tim, Ted turned to Constance. "The car looks clean enough, Mrs Lorimer," he said. "But this is a serious situation and I'm afraid we have to give it a thorough examination. We'll hope to get it back to you tomorrow."

"I'll hope so, too." Mrs Lorimer smiled at Tim. Not triumphantly, she was in control of herself now. But with a quiet confidence which had more over-the-top images bursting about his brain. Including the possibility of someone having put out the operation to contract, even in Guernsey.

Five

Simon Shaw arrived in the detective inspector's office on the dot of eleven. Tim was glad when the time came that he had withstood his impatience to talk to him, and had made the appointment for mid-morning rather than immediately on his arrival at the station: by the time Shaw arrived he had managed to inform those of his colleagues on duty of his unexpected presence and cut out the possibility of shocked reactions at the sight of him at his desk, or stops in corridors while amazement was expressed and he had to go through it all again. The task had been made easier by the comparatively small number of Sunday staff on duty, but with luck the word would have got round by tomorrow morning and he would be stale news.

A few hours on, a bruise was visible on Shaw's left cheek-bone, spreading from under the plaster, and the back of his left hand was black although he had abandoned the sling. Tim, to his surprise, found himself sorry for the boy, and had to force himself into detachment rather than into sympathy, the opposite process to the one he had anticipated.

"Your bruises are coming out. I hope that means they're less painful this morning."

"They're not so bad, I'll be able to do my job." Shaw hesitated. "I've come from the hospital. Lorna had a good night and seems quite cheerful this morning. Shoulder and leg are doing well."

"Yes, I rang her just now and had a chat." He mustn't let himself feel that he and Shaw were rivals in attendance on his mother, for heaven's sake. "But I'm glad to have first-hand evidence that she's doing well. Now— Ah!" The coffee he had ordered to follow Shaw into his office was arriving.

"Despite what's happened since, that was a happy day yesterday," Shaw ventured, when each of them had broached the workmanlike brew. "I'm sorry about Scotland."

"That's the least of it. Yes, it was a happy day. Now," Tim tried again, "my mother will no doubt have told you she's convinced it was Constance Lorimer driving the car last night."

"Oh, she is."

"And you?"

"I only know one side of the Lorimer story, but I did witness Mrs Lorimer's reaction to seeing Lorna yesterday, and it would have to be an extraordinary coincidence if she wasn't the driver."

"Yes. My sergeant and I paid her a visit earlier this morning, and had a look at her car. It's been taken away for professional examination, but on the face of it, from what I could see among its old scars, it was clean. She told us she'd washed it yesterday and we could see it was dry, so unless someone like her crony Beth Smith chooses to let her down, we can hardly say, 'Oh, no, you didn't, you washed it in the early hours of this morning'. Not, from what you and Mother have told me, that a clean car will let her off the hook. You both say your injuries were caused by the impact of falling rather than the impact of the car, and the doctors who saw you bear you out. Which means that washing the car could be enough to remove any evidence of my mother's contact with it. We have to hope for a piece of thread in the tread of a tyre, say. What she was wearing that night has gone to Forensics."

"The policeman at the hospital asked me whether I'd come in contact with the car, and when I said I hadn't he didn't take anything I was wearing. But if you think—"

"No," Tim said, with a sigh. He turned his head a little away from the man the other side of his desk to look out of the window at the huge lime tree dominating the courtyard, a tree that since the CID had joined up with the rest of the island force at the old Town Hospital had in a curious way given him moments of detachment, enabling him to gather his forces when he had something tricky to face. The tree now was lushly beautiful in its yellow-green summer wear, but he found it just as helpful when it was an austere winter skeleton. "Simon," he said, turning back to Shaw, "the possibility does just exist that you could have been the target. In view of your assignment over here."

"It was Lorna in the road!" The reaction was immediate, the sensation of surprise the only sensation showing.

But he had to go on. "I know that. But are you absolutely certain you weren't just in the road, too?"

"Oh, God . . ." Simon ran both hands through his hair, screwing up his face. Tim didn't read his reaction as fear; he thought it came from the man's sudden realisation that he might have been inadvertently inaccurate. "I'd been stepping on and off the pavement, I suppose, looking in the gutter . . . But I was on it most of the time, Lorna having said that was where she expected the other half of her earring to be."

"The car just might have intended to veer your way, then when you ran out to pull Lorna safe the driver didn't bother."

"Seeing her as expendable in his pursuit of me."

"If that was the scenario, then yes. But I appreciate it's much less likely than my mother being the target." Tim leaned across his desk, holding the anxious eyes opposite and affected by them in a way he was unable to explain to himself and pushed impatiently away. "Simon, can you tell me how things have gone to date with your investigation into the Golden Rose? Are they still so far as you know unaware of you and your mission?"

"So far as I know, Tim." The eyes hadn't wavered.

"Can you tell me what you did on Friday?"

"Surely." The hesitation had been brief, and Shaw still hadn't dropped his gaze. "I spent part of the morning with the Town branch of the insurance company – you can check." Tim had matched the ironic smile before reminding himself with a stab of inward irritation that he still knew nothing for certain about the man and that his mother's association with him could be foolish as well as fond even if the insurance company corroborated his story. "And in the afternoon I visited the nursery. I reckoned I might pick up more of the mood of the owners by mingling with the crowd and not having to be furtive than by visiting undercover. Which I may be doing as well, of course." Shaw's eyes dropped to the desk, and Tim wondered if he was contemplating something outside the law: it could explain his anxiety over Tim's policeman's reaction to his profession. "And there was the gossip among the other visitors," Shaw went on, bringing his eyes back to Tim's face. "Sitting in the cafe I overheard quite a few opinions about the fire, and actually saw a man tap his nose and say there's no smoke without it. The place was packed, I suppose some of the crowd was there out of curiosity, there's been so much in the *Press* about the fire, and a bit about the pictures. And as the insurance company are insisting on the greenhouse being left precisely as it ended up while they investigate the claim, the punters can enjoy the thrill of seeing the burnt-out ruin for themselves. It was never open to the public, it's round the private side of the building, so at least it doesn't loom. But it's easily seen and of course people were trekking round just to have a look at it."

"I can imagine. The Golden Rose always attracts a lot of custom, though, because it's a good nursery, even if the Charters haven't personally endeared themselves to Guernsey people."

"They were certainly on the defensive when I saw them. I've burned my boats in one way, Tim, because when I was paying for some cards I told the woman who served me how sorry I was to hear about the fire. I knew she was the owner from the photographs I've been shown, and anyway they don't have assistants, husband and wife both appear to work flat out on their own. The wife was a bit dour, just grunted at my commiserations, but I got the impression she could have been suppressing quite a head of steam. Anxiety? Fear? The idea that she could be afraid came into my mind at the time. The husband, too. I asked him a question about roses and he was quite willing to fill me in but otherwise as unforthcoming as his wife, and I noticed stressed looks between them. There was also the boy, the twelve-year-old son on school holidays, he was moving between his parents and making the odd small sale. He didn't look dour, he didn't look anything, just blank, but my briefing told me that he's slightly withdrawn – not autistic, just a loner who doesn't interact well with other people, especially young people his own age. I noticed the father put an arm round his shoulders a couple of times as if to encourage him, and the boy just gave him a quick look and then went back to what he was doing – arranging some pots, I think."

"Thanks. You did well. It's a pleasure to have an observant

witness who knows how to put his observations into words."
An additional pleasure, because the more Simon Shaw said,
the more Tim felt inclined to believe he really was a private eye
with a brief from a respected insurance company and not likely
to disappear into the blue when he left the office knowing the
police were about to check with the company. "A pity you're
not a grey man." He surveyed the blond locks and handsome
face, and recalled the slim height. "You won't be able to visit
openly again without being remembered here and there."

"I don't think I could get any more than I've got already if
I did. Tim," it was Shaw's turn to lean across his side of the
desk, "I wonder . . . as you haven't gone away . . . Would you
feel able to visit the nursery yourself on some pretext – I don't
mean as a policeman, obviously – and tell me your reactions
to the Charters? It could be very helpful. Look," Shaw went
on, as Tim hesitated, "unless they have a spy in the insurance
company, or in my office, I can't see any way they could – so
far, anyway – know who I am and why I visited the nursery. A
couple of days ago I didn't know a soul in Guernsey, so unless
someone with a grudge against me arising out of my work in
England has followed me here, I don't see how it can be me the
car driver was after. But you'd no doubt like to prove that for
yourself, and visiting the nursery could help you."

"And help *you*. You're asking me to work for you, aren't
you?" Tim asked the question mildly. To his further surprise
he wasn't annoyed by Simon Shaw's disingenuous plea, but he
wanted the man's motive spelled out.

"I'm asking for the opinion of the Guernseyman most quali-
fied to give one. So yes, I suppose I am asking you to work for
me. But investigating crime is your work anyway."

"We've had no reason to doubt the Charters' story. There's
no question of a police investigation of their fire."

"But the insurance company aren't satisfied that their story is the truth. Tim, just an off-duty visit, a few friendly words . . . They know who *you* are, and if they're guilty of anything there could be a wariness, a *something*, about their reaction to you as a policeman which could be an important element in my report. Tim . . ."

"All right." Half an hour ago he would not have believed that Simon Shaw would approach him so boldly, and that he would agree to so impertinent a request. He and Shaw had both changed *vis-à-vis* one another: all the boy could fairly expect of him was suspicion and distaste, yet he had just asked him a huge favour, an action which seemed as totally out of character, so far as Tim had observed Shaw, as it was out of line. And he had agreed to grant it.

There was logic for the change on both sides, though, Tim consoled himself as he glanced at the tree: it was simply that Shaw, seeing such potentially powerful help, had overcome his natural diffidence; and that he, even though he believed it was almost certainly Constance Lorimer who had attempted to run his mother down, would still like either to put the Charters into the frame in Constance's place, or drive them out of the corner of it where they were lurking.

And there was something else, he suddenly recalled, which he could offer Shaw either as an alternative to himself or as an addition. "I've just remembered," he said. "Anna's visited the Charters recently in the line of business; their collie-cross bitch has just had puppies with complications."

"And she'll be going again?" Simon asked eagerly.

"I honestly don't know."

"If she is—"

"You'd like her to keep her eyes and ears open."

"Yes. Look, Tim," Simon said in a rush, "this is an important

64

assignment for me, it could bring more work of the same kind if I'm successful, which would be a wonderful boost to my business. It would be an enormous help if you both could visit."

"Who's in charge of your business while you're away?"

The eyes continued to meet his. "A lady competent enough to direct my two young field operators. But I'm not a very good delegator and I can't help hoping nothing big will crop up until I get back."

"I can understand that." Tim found himself relieved – not, to his surprise, solely on his mother's account – that Shaw appeared to have come clean. "All right, I'll tell Anna what you've told me, and if she's due to see the dogs again and there's anything to spot, she'll spot it."

"I'm sure. I can tell." Shaw got to his feet. "Thank you. Tim . . ." His original diffidence appeared to have come back.

"Yes?" Tim stood up.

"No, it's not another favour, I just want you to know . . . I'm very grateful for your co-operation." Shaw ended on a note of finality, starting to turn towards the door. Tim thought he had set out to say something else.

"We'll both do our best. But my priority is to nail the driver of that car, whoever it was." Tim paused, glancing yet again at the tree as he gathered his forces. Since Shaw had sat down opposite him he had become steadily less inclined for the trial he still felt forced to put him through. "If Constance Lorimer's car is clean, Simon, it won't let her off the hook, but it will make me consider the possibility of the hit-and-run driver being a contract killer." He forced himself to watch Shaw minutely.

"Good God, Tim!" Shaw flopped back into his chair. Tim saw nothing in his face and bearing beyond shock and horror, but he had no idea, for heaven's sake, how good an actor the man was. "You mean Mrs Lorimer . . ."

"Mrs Lorimer, or anyone else. If it was a professional he'll have come and gone within hours so we'll have to look into arrivals and departures." His own professionalism, thank goodness, was forcing him to take it further. "Simon," he said, coming round from behind his desk and stopping in front of Shaw, "do *you* know of anyone else who might want to harm my mother?"

"No!" Shaw was on his feet again, his eyes blazing, his fists clenched. "No, Tim, I don't! Are you trying to say—"

"I'm a policeman, and I'm trying to look at every possibility." With a relief now so strong it surprised him, he was finding Shaw's oblique protestation of innocence convincing. "I don't know how much you see of my mother in England, but if there's anyone there she's afraid of I thought she just might have told you."

"Yes, of course." Shaw sat down again. "Sorry I flew off the handle. You don't know me."

"That's true. Is there anyone in England you feel might have wanted to kill her?"

"Not that I know of. Everyone seems very fond of her. And she's never said anything to me. I swear that's the truth."

"Thank you. Are you intending to go back to the hospital this morning?"

"Well – yes. They've assured me Lorna's ready for visitors."

Even people who aren't family? But he didn't really want to say it aloud. "We may coincide there later, then. Now, my sergeant and I are going to call on Mrs Lorimer's friend Beth Smith. You'll have seen her too yesterday, trying to hold Constance back."

Beth Smith lived in a stout little stuccoed villa towards the other end of the stretch of road culminating in Constance's crumbling Art Deco. Constance had lived there with her husband when he had run away with Lorna, and Tim remembered being driven past the house by his father after his mother had gone, because his father had muttered 'The other poor sod' as they passed. He had been talking to himself, but Tim still had a mental picture of his grandmother putting a restraining hand on his arm, then turning round to smile reassuringly at Tim in the back of the car. He supposed he remembered because it was the only time his father had not been in complete control of himself in his son's company. And his anger had been reserved for Geoffrey Lorimer – Tim had never heard a word said by his father against his mother. Lorimer had died of a heart attack within months of the elopement, and Tim's childish hope that his mother would come back to them had turned into an adult belief that his father would have welcomed her if he hadn't died within a couple of years of her departure, his grandmother said of a broken heart.

Tim had never understood how his mother had been able to leave his father, but in a child's simplistic way, even in the midst of his initial misery at her departure, he had seen it as logical and to be expected that Geoffrey Lorimer – that any man – should prefer her to the squat and unattractive Constance. Even then, he recalled, Constance Lorimer had been charmless. Beth Smith, whom Tim hadn't encountered until she had moved to her present home a few months after his mother's departure, had been tall and fair and soft-voiced, and when she came to the door at noon in answer to DS Mahy's knock he saw, face to face with her, how little changed she was from his childhood image.

"Come in, Mr Le Page. I've been expecting you." She led

him through a hall very different from Constance Lorimer's – white-walled, fresh-smelling, with a gilt-framed mirror and glass shelves carrying ornaments – into a room at the back of the house overlooking the small walled garden in which a young man was at work. Although the old-fashioned french window had been retained the room was still very light, with pale-green chairs and sofa on a pale, faintly green carpet, and there were interesting-looking watercolours on the white walls. Beth Smith, with her looks and taste, must have had a number of suitors, and Tim wondered idly why she had never married. She still looked good, he adjudged, as she turned to him with a smile, and was ageing gracefully: blonde curly hair only a little faded; face, like his mother's, thinning so that the good bones were more prominent; body maintaining its slimness and upright stance. He wondered, less idly, why she was such good friends with Constance Lorimer.

"I won't pretend I don't know why you're here, Inspector Le Page." The voice was soft, slightly breathless. He remembered it as she spoke.

"Thank you. I'll come straight to the point, then." But he hesitated for a moment, approving the immaculately maintained garden in its surround of high stone wall, the support to so many mature climbing plants it was only intermittently visible. "Last night at around midnight a car was driven at my mother in L'Hyvreuse. She was dragged clear, so that although she was hit she wasn't run over. The car didn't slow down, and turned left into Cambridge Park Road."

"Constance told me about your visit to her. And that you think she was the driver," Miss Smith said, as he paused.

"Mrs Lorimer was seen – by myself and other people – to make threatening gestures at Mrs Le Page outside St James yesterday afternoon. You were with her, Miss Smith, and were seen attempting to restrain her. No one else in Guernsey, so far as I am aware, nurses a grudge against my mother."

"Because she took her husband away." Beth Smith spoke almost musingly, looking away from the policeman and staring out at the garden. "It's reason enough for a grudge, Inspector Le Page," she told the french window. "But it doesn't follow she'd attempt a murder."

"She tried to run my mother down thirty years ago, when – before she and Geoffrey Lorimer left the island."

"Thirty years ago!" Beth Smith smiled. "And you think she's cherished murderous intentions over three decades?"

"More to the point," Ted Mahy said, "can you give Mrs Lorimer an alibi for around midnight last night?"

"I wish I could," Miss Smith said sadly. She walked over to a chair and indicated the sofa to Tim and Ted. "I could tell you I was with her," she went on as they sat down, "or she with me, but you'd discover this wasn't true and I might have made things worse for her rather than better."

"Mrs Lorimer told us she didn't take her car out at all yesterday, Miss Smith. Would you be able to corroborate this?"

"I can corroborate that she didn't take it out during the day. We went down to St James by bus, and came back by bus. We had tea at my house, and Constance walked home about nine."

"Did you try to stop her going to see the wedding?" DS Mahy asked.

"Of course. But she was determined. She's been determined ever since she read in the *Press* that Mrs Le Page would be there." Beth Smith paused. "Constance isn't easy to influence. She's well named."

"Yes." Tim glanced for an instant at the peaceful garden before continuing. The young man had straightened up and was resting with his hands on his hips. The way his eyes caressed the french window made Tim recall the island rumour that Beth Smith had a toyboy. "Miss Smith," he said, as he turned back to her, "do you believe Mrs Lorimer could have been driving the car which hit my mother last night?"

She stared at him for a few seconds before replying, her face expressionless. "That's not a fair question, Mr Le Page," she said at last, quietly. "And if your mother hadn't been the victim of last night's hit and run you wouldn't have asked it. I don't think I'm obliged to answer."

"You're not. No." Surprised and ashamed, Tim pulled himself back into professionalism. "I'm sorry."

"I couldn't answer it anyway, could I?" Beth Smith leaned forward in her chair and compelled his eyes to hold her large blue ones. "Constance in her right mind wouldn't consider such a dreadful thing, but who knows how any of us will react under extreme outside pressure?"

Defiantly he blinked. "I would hardly call my mother's presence at my wedding extreme outside pressure, but I take your point, Miss Smith." He and his sergeant got to their feet. "Thank you for your time."

"How is your mother?" she asked him as she rose.

"She'll be all right. Dislocated shoulder. Badly cut leg. Shock. She's getting over them."

"Good. I'm sure Constance will be glad to hear that news, too." Was there irony now in those handsome eyes? If she was guilty, Constance Lorimer would be glad for her own skin as well as for Lorna Le Page's, now that her rage had died.

But had it died? Tim realised how anxious he was for his mother to go back to England.

Six

Tim didn't make it to the Golden Rose that day, but when he learned in the evening from Anna that another visit to the Charters' dogs was scheduled he offered the wary suggestion that she might visit them with two motives, and was agreeably surprised that she immediately accepted. Anna was surprised, too, and smiled a rueful inward smile as she realised why she was welcoming the chance to play a part in Tim's investigation: she had never, in either of her marriages, relished the spotlight that falls on a bride, but as her bridegroom ventured his request she recognised what she hoped was an uncharacteristic sense of grievance that her second tenure of that role had been so quickly upstaged by Lorna's accident.

The evening which should have seen them in Scotland was warm and sunny and still. Tim was aware, as every year he was suddenly aware one day in late summer, of the quality of the sunlight starting to thicken as the sun's arc began to contract towards an autumn still a comfortably long way off. At seven the rays were tangled in the top of his other inspirational tree, the one in his own garden where they were sitting, and it was easy for him to dodge the blinding light and look at his wife in the long chair opposite.

It was the first inactive hour of their day. Anna had spent the morning undoing their honeymoon arrangements, and in the afternoon had been received by the skeleton staff at the

71

practice with overt commiseration and inward relief on what
was turning out to be a busy Sunday. But even in the eventual
peace of the old garden, neither of them could of course relax:
Tim saw Anna's bare brown legs twitch irritably on the seat
rest, and as he watched them she leaned forward to put her
hand over his where it drummed on the wooden arm of his
chair. He found it good to feel her new ring chime against his,
but the unalloyed pleasure of the contact was short-lived.

"Try to think," she said quietly, studying his anxious face.
"Lorna's all right and when she's ready to be discharged she'll
go from the hospital to the airport. We're all right, and we'll
soon be in Scotland."

"When I've brought Constance or whoever to justice."

"I'm glad you said 'or whoever'. That you can still see
Constance as innocent until she's been proved guilty."

"That's why I'm so anxious to prove it."

"Forensics have told you her car's clean, you may not be able
to. You have to accept that, Tim. If ever there's been a case of
cutting one's losses, this is it. The only thing we can be sure of
is getting Lorna safely back to London."

"Constance might follow her."

"All right. We alert the police in England if Constance leaves
Guernsey. Does she leave in the normal way of things?"

"I don't know. I suppose she goes on holiday."

"I gather she didn't follow your mother when she carried her
husband off the island?"

"No."

"But she did try to run her down before they left. Did she
own up to that?"

"She had to. She crashed into a hedge and was unable to drive
off so she could hardly deny it. I was very small, but I remember
my mother laughing."

"Constance would have known where to find your mother then. And she knew where to find her now, with the where and the when of her visit being advertised in the *Press*. If it was Constance who drove at your mother last night that could have been because fate had given her a second irresistible opportunity, and we can make sure she never gets a third. Anyway, she's tasted blood this time, so let's hope she finds that enough. If she did it, Tim. We have to keep saying that like a refrain."

"I know. I try. There *is* one idea that makes it easier, but I don't want . . ."

"Yes?" He had tailed off, and Anna saw the anxiety in his face as he dropped his eyes and leaned down to pluck a long stem of grass.

"Nothing. Forget it." Tim manoeuvred the grass between his thumbs and blew a piercing blast. "An old trick, I haven't tried it for years. Let's have another drink." He levered himself out of his deep chair and collected the two tall glasses from the grass.

It was the first time since they had got to know one other that Anna had been aware he had thought better of confiding in her. By the time the cold realisation had released her it seemed too late to persist. "Are you hungry?" she heard herself asking.

"No," Tim said, considering in surprise. Eating seemed to be something he had forgotten about.

"Nor me, but I'll eventually get something together."

His short absence was an opportunity to try to rationalise his rebuff. "Now," she said, when Tim was back in his chair and they had both sampled their refills, "Cliff was going to visit the Golden Rose for me tomorrow. When I go in in the morning I'll tell him I'll do it. It's natural enough, I saw the bitch through the birth." She raised her glass. "Here's to justice, darling!"

73

Anna had expected this weekend, of all the weekends of her life, to be lived under the constant gaze of the man she had just married, but Tim was staring distractedly into the branches of the tree above him, and she had to repeat herself before he heard her and lowered his eyes.

"Yes," he said flatly. "To justice."

"What is it, Tim?" Suddenly she had to venture. "What did you almost say just now?"

"I almost said . . . What if the car was coming for *him*, but he pushed *her* forward?"

"She'd have known. She's been so grateful that he pulled her back."

"Which he could have done the instant the impact was over. Oh, I don't know. In different circumstances I think I'd like him. I want to believe what he tells me. But I can't quite manage it."

The next day the weather was still set fair, and the blackened ruin of the greenhouse that had served as an extension to the Charters' rambling old house stood out shockingly under the cloudless blue sky. The nearest bushes were singed amber, but the unnaturally coloured circle scarcely eased the contrast with the general surround of prime trees and bushes in full summer leaf and flower. Normally Anna would have driven beyond the car-park and stopped outside the house door, but today she parked with the public and walked through the indoor sales area, expanding under the Charters into a place where more and more people now went to buy non-floral presents. It was still small scale, she noted, as it would have to be while the owners worked it entirely themselves, but the choice and arrangement of the objects for sale showed an assured talent for exploiting the retail gift market. The Charters would have

74

been glad to sell their valuable pictures, if only to take on more staff . . .

When Marjorie Charters answered the bell she wasn't quite quick enough in changing her expression from alarm to relief to blankness: Anna noted each swift transition, and that her thin face had grown gaunt, the pale skin with a yellow tinge under eyes that seemed larger and darker than Anna recalled them, her flyaway fair hair looking dishevelled now rather than fashionably tousled. But it could be she was seeing what Simon Shaw's mission had encouraged her to expect to see. And didn't want to see, she realised with a flash of pity, even though proof of fraud by the Charters would give Shaw the boost he craved . . . Not for the first time, Anna wondered at Tim's comparative indulgence of Simon Shaw.

"Good afternoon, Mrs Weston." Marjorie Charters' voice was as weary as her appearance. "Or Mrs Le Page, I should be saying," she went on in the same monotone. "I saw the notice of your wedding to the detective inspector in the *Press*. Our congratulations. But I thought you would be on your honeymoon. I was expecting Mr Ozanne." No curiosity in the dull eyes, but that could as well be that her thoughts were elsewhere as that she knew why the bridal couple had stayed at home. And Anna had already observed enough of both husband and wife to be convinced that neither of them was stupid.

"We were, Mrs Charters." She blessed the bitch for her timely arrival, running out through the kitchen door with gold-fronded tail furiously waving. Response to her with fondling and loving looks would help to disguise a close scrutiny of her owner as she told her the news. "But on Saturday night my mother-in-law was knocked down in L'Hyvreuse by a hit-and-run driver. Fortunately she was dragged clear of the wheels but she's cut her leg badly and dislocated her shoulder.

And she's very shocked, of course. So naturally we haven't gone away."

"Oh, I am sorry!" There was a hint of concern in the voice now, but that could be no more than a reflex of good manners. Anna studied Marjorie Charters' face in the intervals of her apparent engagement with the dog, and saw none of the surprise a guilty woman who was also clever would surely have feigned. "In the Princess Elizabeth, is she?" The high pale brow had creased before the question was asked, as if Mrs Charters was having to force her attention onto a matter outside her own concerns. Anna reminded herself that the loss of the pictures and the greenhouse was misfortune enough to dry up what at the best of times, she had suspected before that morning, would be a small stock of empathy.

"Yes. She'll be all right, but she'll be there for a few days."

There was no further response, and after another word with the dog Anna straightened up and looked over to the ruin. "The *Press* said you lost some valuable pictures. I'm so sorry." That was all the *Press had* said. If Bernard Charters, in his apparent anguish, hadn't blurted the information out to the media they wouldn't have said that much. Unless, of course, Anna reflected, the amateur critic Henry Thomas had had a word with them. Judging by the little the *Press* had printed, he appeared to have kept quiet. But the Charters must have known he could talk, and if they were guilty of fraud they would surely have thought it politic to pre-empt him. Which could mean that Bernard Charters' outburst had been calculated . . .

Alarm again, as quickly gone. "Yes." Marjorie Charters spoke calmly, holding Anna's concerned gaze until the boy came running out of the doorway behind her and stopped dead at the sight of the visitor, so abruptly Anna imagined the squealing of brakes. He looked questioningly up at his mother, his eyes huge with apprehension.

"You know Mrs Weston," Marjorie said, putting an arm round his shoulders. "She's come to see Beauty. You're going to have to get used to calling her Mrs Le Page, she got married yesterday." The warmth of real awareness of someone else's disaster at last came into her face, reminding Anna that the first time she had met Marjorie Charters she had thought her attractive. "Heavens, how awful for you! The very night . . ."

"Yes. It *was* awful." She was going to take a gamble. "The worst thing is that it happened in L'Hyvreuse, outside the Duke of Richmond where my mother-in-law's been staying. Whoever it was drove up from the lookout and so couldn't have been travelling at any speed unless they deliberately put their foot down."

"But . . ." The horror and disbelief were just what was to be expected from an innocent listener. "You're saying . . . Deliberately . . . But Mr Le Page's mother doesn't even live on the island, how could someone here—"

"Disturbed people have been known to hit out at anyone who happens to be around." Marjorie Charters hadn't been in Guernsey long enough to know about an old scandal which until the early hours of yesterday morning had appeared to be dead and buried. And anyway, Anna reminded herself, if she and her husband were guilty of the attack, it wasn't Lorna they had been after.

"Yes . . . She didn't see who it was, then?"

"No."

It was impossible to tell if there had been anxiety behind the question, or if there was relief at the negative reply. "You said someone pulled her to safety?"

"Yes." This question could mean innocence, or the extreme

77

boldness of guilt. "So the car didn't actually go over her. But she's very shocked."

"Of course . . ." Marjorie Charters' concern appeared to be reverting inwards. She looked down at the boy, still in the crook of her arm, his curiously light and now expressionless eyes fixed openly and without embarrassment on Anna's face.

"What are you going to do today, Benjamin? Why not ring one or two of your friends from school and ask them to come over?"

The boy jerked impatiently, returning his gaze to his mother. "I'm going to draw. I don't want any friends from school. Can I use the end of the new greenhouse where there aren't any plants? Please!" He tugged at his mother's sleeve.

"All right," Marjorie Charters said, studying his face. "For the time being."

"I'll take one of the trestle tables!" he said, on an excited gulp of breath. He broke away from his mother, running his hands through his spiky dark hair as he set off the way Anna had come. "And I can put my things in that cupboard," he shouted, turning as he was about to disappear round the angle of the building. "There's lots of room." His stocky body broke into a run.

"He's self-sufficient for his age," Marjorie murmured, staring after him. Struggling now, Anna thought, to keep her anxiety out of her face. She wondered if Marjorie's optimistic summing-up of her son was for her own morale as well as for the information of her visitor.

"He plays a lot on his own, then?" she asked casually, resuming her fondling of the useful dog, whose cold damp noise was nudging at her hand for attention.

"Yes." There was a faint air of belligerence in the monosyllable, as if Marjorie Charters was challenging Anna to tell her that solitary play was unusual or unhealthy. "I think it's good

78

for an only child to be that way, not relying all the time on other people to make his amusement."

Not relying any of the time, Anna suspected, from her observation of the boy as well as from what she had heard from a few different people.

"He'll be missing his study space in the burned greenhouse," she suggested. Benjamin had once taken her to see it. "But I suppose you'll have the greenhouse rebuilt when the insurance company pays up." Anna smiled as she spoke, trying to look innocent and encouraging, and then trying not to show her satisfaction that Marjorie Charters had stiffened, the length of her body, to wary attention.

"Yes! And that won't be long!" she said sharply. "Let me take you to the pups."

"Of course." As she followed Mrs Charters into the kitchen, Anna knew she had got all she could hope for.

The puppies, including the runt, were doing well, and a quarter of an hour later she was getting into her car and answering her mobile.

"Anna? Can you come to the Princess Elizabeth?"

"Tim?"

"It's all right. Mother's all right, but she wants . . . Can you come?"

It might be all right, but he sounded upset. "Something's wrong."

"Not exactly. But I'd like to see you here, if you can possibly manage it."

"It was never more convenient, I'm just leaving the Golden Rose. Not entirely without profit."

"Good." It sounded mechanical. "I'll see you in a moment, then."

Perversely, Monday was turning out to be considerably less

busy than the understaffed Sunday, and the rest of her afternoon allowed space for the unexpected. Anna went straight to the hospital.

Lorna was sitting in her armchair, dressed to go out and looking composed and determined as well as almost restored to elegance. Tim was pacing the room and looking frustrated and cross. Both appealed immediately to Anna as she crossed the threshold.

"Anna, darling, tell this stuffy old son of mine . . ."

"Anna, for goodness' sake, help me talk some sense into Mother . . ."

"Please!" Anna sat down on the bed. "What's this all about?"

The second dual outburst was won by Lorna, as Tim gave way with a frustrated waving of his arms and, breathing heavily, sank down beside Anna.

"I'm feeling quite well and strong again, and I'm going to face Constance Lorimer. That's all. But this son of mine—"

Tim was back on his feet. "I popped in to see her, and found her ordering a taxi. Anna, can't *you* make her see what a ridiculous—"

"I don't behave ridiculously," Lorna said, with an enormous dignity only slightly diminished by her finding herself unable to stand without the support of the chair arm. "And I'm going to see Constance. I've agreed to go home straight from this hospital, Anna, and Constance is hardly likely to attack me again. At the moment, anyway."

"For God's sake, Mother!"

"I need to see her, Tim. I'm so angry. I don't show it, so you probably don't realise, men only realise things they can see or hear or touch or smell. I'm not going to make a scene, I'm just going to tell her quietly and with dignity that she's the lowest form of human life ever created."

80

"Dear God," Tim moaned, but Anna was watching Lorna's face and seeing in every straining muscle the evidence that she would be unable to rest until she had had her say.

"Look, Tim." She got to her feet and stood in front of him, forcing his pacing to a stop and putting her hands on his arms. "It looks to me as if your mother has got to do this."

"*Et tu, Brute!*"

"No. Listen. I can understand."

"But we don't know that Constance was driving that car. As you've kept on telling me."

"All right." She put aside for the moment the fact that he had never before spoken to her sarcastically. "But that's not how your mother sees it. She's convinced it was Constance—"

"Of course it was Constance!" Lorna moved towards them, away from the support of her chair, and Anna took her arm as unobtrusively as possible. "Thank you, Anna, you *do* understand." The dazzle of Lorna's smile was fully restored. "I have to have my say, and I have to have it now."

"Yes. Will you let me drive you?"

"For God's sake!" Tim hit his head against a wall.

"And go in with you? As far as Constance Lorimer is concerned I'm neutral, I won't affect your confrontation."

"Yes!" Lorna said promptly. "If it's the only way I can get you to take me."

Tim was pacing again, and Anna held out her other hand and seized him by the arm as he was striding past. "It'll be all right," she said, as she strengthened her grip. "And we might learn something from Mrs Lorimer's reactions."

Tim ceased to strain against Anna's grasp, in his face, suddenly, the brooding concentration she had noted before when he was contemplating a possible work breakthrough. "We just might, yes . . ." he murmured. "If you'll stay with

81

her," he ended severely. Anna suspected him of chastising himself without knowing it for having briefly forgotten that he was personally involved in the problem he was facing.

"Of course."

"All right, then. But I'm not happy."

"I think it's more important, at this moment, for your mother to do what makes *her* happy. I'm sorry, Tim," Anna continued swiftly, as she saw the disgruntled surprise in his face. And perhaps she *had* been paying him back even while saying what she believed. "But if Lorna doesn't go and see Mrs Lorimer I don't think she'll be able to put all this behind her."

"That's it precisely. You're a jewel, Anna." Lorna kissed Anna's cheek, then stroked Tim's arm. "It'll be all right, darling. Try not to worry so much."

"Easier said than done." But resignation was now apparent in Tim's every line. "At least try to be careful what you say. Especially if Beth Smith or someone's there who can be a witness to an outright accusation."

"It'll be all right, Tim." Anna was shocked to find herself afraid as she took Tim's hand that it might repulse hers, and it was a relief when it responded and his fingers meshed with hers.

"You're not leaving, Lorna!"

Simon Shaw was in the doorway, and Tim's hand convulsed.

"Only temporarily, Simon. I'm going to visit Constance Lorimer, as I told you I would."

This time Tim's hand clenched so strongly round his wife's that she murmured a protest. But she had understood: Tim's mother had told her boyfriend what she had not told him, and the painful gesture was a reflex response to his hurt and anger.

Tim understood his reaction, too, and was shocked by it. "I'm sorry, darling," he murmured in response.

"It's all right." In a rare public gesture, Anna rubbed her cheek against his. "And it'll be all right if I'm with her."

"Maybe." Tim turned to Simon. "Anna's taking Lorna to Mrs Lorimer. I'm sorry your visit has to be so short." He didn't like himself for enjoying saying that, either. And he didn't like the sudden recollection that his new sourness had come upon him since he had become a married man. The moment his mother was safely off to England he and Anna must be off to Scotland.

Seven

O ne or two white puffs of cloud were hanging now in the blue sky, but the sun still shone as serenely as it had shone all day, and as they turned north on to the coast road to wind their way up to St Sampson Anna's spirits lifted as they lifted inevitably whenever she reached the sea. She could be apprehensive about a professional visit, afraid of what she might find or what she might have to do, but sight of the sea, never more than moments away in whichever direction she drove and presenting an infinity of aspects, filled her always with elation, whatever she was dreading. Even the prospect of her present destination, and her alarmingly uncertain role when she reached it, failed to arrest the leap of her heart when suddenly before them was the blue-grey water stretching out of sight to a hazy horizon, shot with silver where the sun caught its lazy wavelets. On this eastern stretch of coast between Guernsey's two towns it was a pale backdrop to business, most of its boundary with the land marked by austere stone wall, rather than the royal-blue plaything it would be today in the west . . .

"She'll be drinking tea," Lorna was saying, yawning and stretching, then grunting with pain as her injuries reminded her of their existence. "The bitch," she added between her teeth as she looked down at her bandaged leg. "She always had tea at four o'clock, with a gipsy cream or a bourbon. When we got to England Geoffrey said he never wanted to see a standard sweet biscuit again. A creature of habit, Constance. Well, she won't be able to make a habit of driving her car at me because I won't be around." But Lorna sighed, not sounding as satisfied as her words made out. "This island is rather special, though, isn't it?"

"I wouldn't want to live anywhere else, now. Friends from England say they can't understand why I don't feel claustrophobic, living on a piece of land seven miles long by four miles wide, and I say how could I, only a few minutes in every direction from infinite space. You're a Guern, Lorna. Do you really not miss it?"

"Of course I miss it. Part of me will always belong here. But I had to go, once, and now I couldn't come back."

"Your son's here."

Lorna gave a strange little laugh, evoking another grunt of pain. "Yes. But there are – things – in England I wouldn't want to leave. Anna . . ."

"Yes?"

"Take the next turning left, dear. I'll need to direct you from now on." Anna suspected that directions were not what Lorna a moment earlier had set out to give her. "It's not a bad road," Lorna said grudgingly, after their third turn, "but then of course it was Geoffrey who chose the house. And bought the period contents, which he told me amused him at the time. And I imagine it avoided a lot of rows, Constance has no aesthetic sense. I don't suppose he envisaged them still being in place another thirty years on, but I shan't be surprised if they are. Not that I can make comparisons, this will be the first time I've set foot in the house. Anna!" Lorna said with sudden sharpness. "Pull up here for a moment. I want a few deep breaths."

"A few second thoughts?"

"Certainly not. I'm going to confront Constance Lorimer."

"Why did Geoffrey marry her?" Even allowing for Lorna's inevitable prejudice, Anna had heard nothing positive about Constance as a wife from anyone else who had spoken of her, and a sudden sharp curiosity overcame the shortness of her acquaintance with her mother-in-law as well as her native diffidence.

"Why do you think?" The scornful rhetoric, too resonant for the confined space, reminded Anna that before marrying Tim's father Lorna had been briefly on the stage. "She told him she was pregnant and he believed her. How he ever . . . Well, it was on a plate, of course, and he was young and society then made it difficult for the young unmarried to get sex. Geoffrey was an honourable man, Anna, it's important for me that you as well as Tim should believe that, and he married her. There was no pregnancy, of course. I don't think there ever had been. She couldn't even give him a baby."

"So it wasn't Geoffrey—"

"No!" Another sharp gesture, another bitten-off yelp of pain. "And you must be thinking it wasn't the action of an honourable man to leave his wife, but she gave him a dog's life. She never wanted to go out, she never interested herself in anything he cared about or did, or cared about or did anything herself, including keeping her house in order and making proper meals. And you don't have to take just my word for that, everyone was sorry for him. Even if he and I hadn't met he'd eventually have had to get away from Constance. Nobody blamed him." Lorna had been talking to herself, Anna fancied, seeing the past through the windscreen where her eyes stared unblinking, but now she turned to Anna with an ironic smile. "They blamed *me* though, of course. But then, I had left another good man. Tim's father. The best news I could have had from the island would

86

have been that he had found a good woman. But he never did."
Lorna sighed again. "I expect you wonder why I left him, don't
you? Unless Tim has offered you an explanation."

"He hasn't. And yes, of course I wonder."

"I think perhaps we knew each other too well. We were
friends when we were children, then I went to England and
– and I thought I'd got it all out of my system. But I hadn't,
Anna. Between my marriage and meeting Geoffrey there were
other men."

"Tim did hint that much."

"You know," Lorna said lightly, "I sometimes think that if
I'd known Geoffrey as a child and met Edward as a woman, it
could have happened the other way round."

"Geoffrey died, didn't he, not long after you went to
England?" Anna asked warily.

"Yes. He had a heart attack. So no doubt Constance thinks of
me as a murderer as well as a husband snatcher. Which could
just explain what she's tried to do – an eye for an eye."

"Yes, I can see that. Lorna . . . Did you never think . . . Was
there never a chance of going back to Tim's father?"

"You can appear diffident," Lorna said, turning to smile
ironically at Anna. "But you aren't. I thought of it, yes, and
perhaps I would have tried if he hadn't died, too, a couple
of years later." Lorna turned away and pointed through her
window. "Just ahead, that's Beth Smith's house. Now, *she*'s
been loyal to Constance, I can't think why."

"Even Constance can't be all bad, Lorna. The house looks
nice." It was a villa of Tim's vintage, smaller and pink-stuccoed
where Tim's was white, and with a deeper and attractively
planted front garden.

"Oh, Beth's got style. And she's bright. I can't think why
she never found a man. Unless she's not interested in them. I

used to wonder sometimes, she always seemed to be so hostile to Geoffrey."

"Island rumour has it that she's got – a boyfriend." Anna had been going to describe him as young, but remembered Simon in time.

"Good luck to her." Anna could feel Lorna struggling to pull herself upright. "Well, we'd better get on with it."

"You really are sure you want to confront Mrs Lorimer?"

"Of course. I have to let her know what I think of her. And don't tell me please that she's likely to know already. Certain things need restating from time to time. Especially when there's been grievous bodily harm. Oh, Anna!" Lorna shouted to the back of the house. "I'm so angry! All right, I know how I would have felt if another woman had taken Geoffrey away from *me* – not that any woman could have done – but I'd have got on with things eventually, I wouldn't have brooded my life away and I certainly wouldn't have tried to destroy the woman who had won. Stop by that lamp-post. Are you sure you wouldn't prefer to wait outside?" Lorna asked, as for the second time they slid to a halt.

"I would prefer to, but I'm not going to. You're not well enough yet to stand on your own physically and you don't want to have to collapse into a chair. I won't cramp your style." Anna hoped she had not just given an undertaking she would find impossible to honour. "And if Mrs Lorimer brings an action for slander it'll be useful to have an independent record of what was said."

She could have said too much. Anna held her breath, but to her relief Lorna threw her an amused glance. "You make it difficult to know how far your tongue is into your cheek, Anna. I admire that. Now, perhaps you'll go round and help me out."

The process was hampered by Lorna's reaction to the sight of Constance Lorimer's house, a mingling of shock and satisfaction that had her falling back into her seat. "I didn't expect it to be *that* bad," she said wonderingly, when she was eventually upright on the pavement and holding Anna's arm. "She can't have done a thing to it since Geoffrey left."

"It looks like she could be going to pieces," Anna responded. "You'll really have to be careful, Lorna."

"So will you, Anna." Lorna gave her a dazzling smile. "Please don't offer me any more advice."

"I'm sorry." She had presumed too much and it was another shock, sharper than the shock of the dilapidated pile in front of them. "Such a lot has happened since we met I keep forgetting I've known you so short a time."

"Well, that's good." To Anna's relief, the hand emerging from the sling across Lorna's chest gave her arm a feeble pat. "I feel the same. That's why I came back on you the way I come back on Tim. Neither of you can tell me what to do about Constance Lorimer. Come on."

Lorna pulled Anna towards the once black wooden gate, now cracked down one side and off the lower of its two rusty hinges. The short concrete path was cracked too, the fissures marked here and there by growths of weeds which were the only healthy-looking things within sight, and the metal surface of the grid pattern on the two wide curved windows to each side of the scarred front door was more rust than yellow paint. There were putty-coloured pits in the grey pebbledash, and Anna found herself surprised when the old-fashioned stud bellpush evoked a shrill ring from within.

"Does Beth Smith have no influence?" Anna whispered.

Lorna shrugged her uninjured shoulder. "If she sees Constance as her foil, she may like her this way."

A wavering and fuzzy-edged second circle had appeared above the glass sunburst in the top part of the door, and there was a grinding sound as the door shook for a few seconds before jolting inwards. Constance Lorimer's head would not have reached the sunburst, and Anna was prepared for the sight of the tall Beth Smith.

Lorna, too, appeared ready for Constance's friend. "Miss Smith!" There could have been a slight emphasis on the first word. "I've come to see Constance. This is my daughter-in-law Mrs Le Page, as you will know from your presence on Saturday at my son's wedding. I need her arm at the moment because of the injuries I sustained later that day. May we come in, please? Ah! Constance!"

A squat figure, cigarette in hand, was hovering in the doorway of one of the front rooms, frowning at what must be the two featureless dark shapes against the dazzle through the open front door. Beth Smith stood aside in silence, and Anna and Lorna advanced into the hall. Still arm in arm with her mother-in-law, Anna felt Lorna's chest heave and heard her catch of breath before the retch rose in her own throat and she managed to subdue it with a cough. Constance Lorimer's hall smelt terrible, and piercing the staleness of dust, tobacco and old food there was a sharp note of decay. Damp rot at least, Anna adjudged as she tried to wipe her wet eyes unobtrusively, if not the faster growing kind.

"What are you doing here, Lorna Le Page?"

The voice was deep for a woman, the voice of a lifelong female smoker, and Anna welcomed the smell of fresh tobacco as a comparative cleanser of the olfactory cocktail she was hoping Lorna at least would get used to sufficiently to do herself justice. Surely Beth Smith didn't eat food prepared in Constance Lorimer's kitchen?

"Do you really have to ask me that, Constance?"

"Yes, I do." The response was prompt and sharp. "So you'd better tell me. Come in!"

She made an impatient gesture, then led the way into the room from which she had emerged as they arrived, toiling along as if her hips were painful. It was only then that Beth Smith shut the front door, and Anna suspected she had been attempting to lessen the impact of the interior of her friend's house on people entering it for the first time.

The room into which Constance led them had a transom window open and was slightly less odiferous than the hall. Anna realised to her relief that she had regained control of her throat. As Lorna had alerted her, the room had been furnished to match the architectural style of the house, and the creamy white which had been so popular as a background to Art Deco – plain stippled walls, unpatterned carpet, three-piece suite – was still grubbily in place.

"You'd better sit down, Mrs Le Page," Constance suggested, when she had looked Lorna up and down. She had planted her slippered feet a little apart in front of a once-white fireplace decorated with intermittent slabs of malachite, towards which she flicked her ash backwards without turning round, and Anna had a fantasy that she was a mushroom growth attached to the floor, nurtured by the damp below and around her. And the skin of her face and hands was the colour of fungus, supporting the illusion. Searching for something to explain Geoffrey Lorimer's youthful indiscretion, Anna saw that his wife's hair was still dark, wavy and abundant, the sort of hair that however much neglected can never look too badly untidy or unkempt, and that in the mushroom-coloured face there glittered a pair of huge and beautiful brown eyes.

"I prefer to stand, thank you," Lorna responded, to Anna's

relief still in a temperate tone of voice. And she was relaxed enough to squeeze Anna's arm and nod towards the mug on the low mantelshelf half full of a mahogany-coloured liquid.

"As you please. Now—"

"I'll sit down, Constance. Unless you prefer me to leave the room." Beth Smith made a token move towards the door.

"Mrs Le Page and I have nothing confidential to say to one another. Nothing to say at all, unless she has come to apologise thirty years late. So sit down, Beth, by all means."

"Apology *is* connected with my visit, Mrs Lorimer," Lorna said, as Beth Smith, in a graceful gesture, sat down on the edge of the armchair nearest to the door. Anna had felt Lorna's reaction as Constance spoke in the trembling of her arm, and it was another stab of relief to hear her continue to speak calmly. "I would like an apology from you for your attempt to kill me on Saturday night. After you have given me an explanation of why you drove your car at me for a second time."

"I didn't drive my car at you, Mrs Le Page."

"Or perhaps I'll give *you* one," Lorna continued, as if there had been no response. "Unless you are ill you must have known that you couldn't get away with it. So you must be ill. And as your illness is making you violent, you obviously need to be restrained. I shall speak to the police before I leave the island."

Lorna sustained her slow, quiet tone to the end of her speech, but Anna was aware of the increasing tremor of her body.

"A word to your son?" Constance Lorimer rasped scornfully. "Don't waste your energies, Mrs Le Page." *I am still the one who is Mrs Lorimer*. Anna heard the subtext as clearly as if it had been spoken aloud. "The police have just returned my car, which of course showed no signs of an accident it wasn't involved in. I didn't drive at you on Saturday night, but I can believe from what I know of you that there must be a number of people who might well have done. And that's what I'll tell whoever you set on me."

"Constance, dear . . ." Beth Smith murmured.

"Oh, let her say what she wants to say, Miss Smith. It's so crazy it's almost entertaining." Lorna imposed a brief look of amusement on to her tense face. "Which is more than I can say for her house. I wonder you can visit such a pigsty; five minutes in it has been enough for me."

"Be careful, Mrs Le Page." Constance Lorimer's voice had sunk to a growl. "Remember there is a law of libel and slander." *Yes, please remember*, Anna begged in her head, grateful for the warning she herself could not have dared to give.

Lorna gave a choking cough Anna suspected of being contrived because it was the only face-saving way of dealing with her adversary's return threat. "I can't stay here any longer," she said, after ostentatiously wiping her eyes. "And I've said what I came to say. I know you tried to kill me on Saturday, Constance, and I believe that only someone who is mentally ill can nurse a hatred so strong it survives three decades intact. Let's go, Anna."

"Yes, go, Mrs Le Page. And go carefully."

Constance Lorimer's fierce eyes could have been glaring through a mask, they were the only points of life in her inert bloodless face. She made no move from where she was planted, feeding Anna's fantasy that she was a vegetable growth, and it was Beth Smith who rose from her chair in another graceful gesture and led the way out into the hall and swiftly across to the front door, which she immediately opened.

Lorna started to gulp in air, then asked Miss Smith how she could stand it.

"Constance and I have been friends a long time." The voice

was soft and light, but Miss Smith lowered it as she went on. "And now she needs me. I don't know whether or not she tried to injure you, Mrs Le Page, she denies it to me, too, but I *am* worried about her state of mind." Miss Smith paused, her large blue eyes troubled. "I don't want to upset you, particularly when you're not well, but I don't think she has ever properly recovered from Geoffrey's departure. She was never outgoing, but she's become more and more reclusive, especially in the last few years."

"She's lucky to have a friend like you."

Beth Smith, after a glance towards the open sitting-room door, led the way out of the house. "Don't make too much of that," she said, coming to a stop halfway along the short path to the gate. "I have other friends and other interests. And when Constance and I eat together, it's either in a restaurant or at my house. Now, I must go back to her. She may not have shown it, but she'll be very upset."

"I didn't show it either, did I?" Lorna demanded, when they were in the car and Anna was struggling to fasten her passenger's seatbelt. "But I'm very upset too."

"You did well. Which doesn't mean I wasn't worried—"

"Beth Smith wasn't taking notes and I don't suppose there was a tape running in that terrible room." Lorna took a deep breath and sank down into her seat. "I feel better for that, Anna. Do you have to go back to work?"

"I've no more visits today, but I'd like to look in at the surgery before the day's out." Anna glanced at the clock. "Say by half-past five. And anyway I think you should be back at the hospital by then. So we've got almost an hour. Would you like a nostalgic drive around?"

"I'd love it."

"Any special place?"

94

"Geoffrey and I used to go north to L'Ancresse, there's so much space there. I remember running about on the grass, not going anywhere, just trying to run away from tension. It happened with Geoffrey and me during the autumn and winter, and sometimes at L'Ancresse we could feel we were the only people in the world and that everything was easy. It won't be like that on a fine summer's day, and I can't run or walk, so let's just park on the common and open the windows. There used to be cows tethered along the grass verge by the Route de l'Ancresse," Lorna observed wistfully as they set off. "And even in the rough between the golf course fairways. Lovely barrel-bodied ginger Guernsey cows."

"There still are."

They came across two lying down and two grazing. Cars carrying yellow Hs for 'Hire' held them up as tourists in front of them slowed down for their children to lean out of windows and call delightedly to the indifferent beasts.

Between golf course and common Anna turned seawards. Two martello towers stood sentinel on the course itself at the back of L'Ancresse Bay, and their road ended at the foot of another, at a car-park which like so many in Guernsey's coastal places was a natural stony plateau, scarcely adapted. The park was still nearly full, but there was a space facing the sea. "There must be more martello towers here than anywhere else on the island," Anna commented as the tyres crunched into it. "Tim calls them nice, crumbly-textured cabinet puddings."

"I know. He's tended since childhood to go in for strained and/or culinary metaphors." Lorna smiled reminiscently. "Because of the coast in the north being at sea level and sandy it was reckoned to be the most vulnerable part of the island to invasion by Napoleon. Hence the cluster of towers. And Fort Marchant out on the headland in front of us. Geoffrey and I used to go there." Lorna sighed again as she wound her window down, and the freshness of the sea crept into the car without cooling the warm air. "Guernsey tips north which is why we have all those spectacular cliffs in the south and those coy little bays so hard to reach. But I like the generosity of the coast up here and the huge feeling of space. Even the grey of the rocks. Have you noticed how the rocks change colour as you move along the coast? On the south and west coasts they're pink and thousands of years older than the grey north. Don't look so surprised, Anna." Lorna burst out laughing. "I was bright at school and very interested in the strange little place where I'd been born."

"You miss it, don't you?"

"Of course. Especially on a day like this."

The clouds had disappeared but the featureless blue sky was paling towards evening, beginning to draw colour out of the blue sea and the tree-belted green land stretched wide behind the bay. The curved yellow beach of L'Ancresse Bay ahead of them, and the edge of the lapping tide, were still speckled with people, but some of them were packing up, and as Anna and Lorna lapsed into silence two adults and three children wreathed in beach equipment came laggingly up to their car.

"Has Simon told you how his assignment's going?" Anna asked, when they had watched the slow process of loading up and seen the family drive off.

"No. But he never does."

"I had to visit the Charters' dogs this afternoon, and I talked as much about the fire as I felt I could without making Marjorie Charters suspicious. She's certainly very tense. But I suppose with so much money at stake . . . They seem very ambitious about the business."

"I'm afraid, Anna," Lorna said in a rush.

"Constance won't dare to try anything else."

"No . . . I suppose it's Constance I'm afraid of, but . . . I hope Simon won't do anything rash."

For an instant, before Lorna's face went blank, Anna saw in it a mingling of concern and affection that convinced her of something she would not tell Tim: his mother loved the young man she had brought with her to his wedding.

Eight

"I want you to go to Scotland!" Lorna announced later that evening, when she was resting on her hospital bed and Anna and Tim were seated each side of her. "I'm fine now but I'll stay here until I leave Guernsey, and I promise I won't do that until they're ready to discharge me."

"No more visits to Constance Lorimer, Mother?"

"I've no more to say to her. The only visit I shall make, darlings, is into the past if Simon has time to take me on another run around."

"Is he still intending to leave on Wednesday?" Anna asked, after waiting a moment to give Tim the chance he didn't take.

"Probably. But I don't expect to be far behind him."

"You live alone," Tim said. Anna wondered if his statement was really a question. "Which could make the hospital decide you should convalesce here rather than at home."

"So I'll still be here when you get back from Scotland. I think I can cope with that, darling. One week."

"I don't know . . ."

"Please go. I'll feel much less guilty if you get your marriage trip, and I can think about you in Scotland together. I'm stocked up with paperbacks, and there's the TV and nice doctors and nurses to talk to. Please try first thing in the morning to book for as soon as there are vacancies. Anna!"

"Lorna means it, Tim. So – if you still want to?"

"Of course."

But Anna was cold because of Tim for the second time since he had become her husband, seeing the hesitation in his eyes. "All right. I'll see in the morning what I can do."

They drove home in silence, but as they stopped on the short slope up to the garage door Tim put his hand on Anna's. "I do want to go to Scotland, darling. Be alone with you where no one can get at us. It's just . . . Part of me feels there's unfinished business here and that I ought to be on the spot to clear it up."

Infinitely solaced, Anna twisted her hand upwards and laced his fingers. "I understand." She was shocked that she had questioned her happiness. "But there really isn't anything you can do about Constance Lorimer. Or about anything Simon Shaw might have tried to do. Awful as the thought is, he'll have a free hand when they're back in England. But you don't really think he tried to hurt her, do you?"

"I don't suppose so. The worst I can think, really, is that if he was the target of the car he hid behind her. Which would make him a wretch of the first order but not a would-be killer. No, I can't do anything here. Let's try and get away."

She kissed his cheek. "Let's. Ah. Whitby."

The large middle-aged tabby cat was vaulting gazelle-like on to the bonnet of the car, and rode on it into the garage when Tim had opened the doors, according to his nightly habit if he happened to be around when the car came home. As usual he changed places with Duffy as the front door was opened, and was sitting upright by the fridge when they entered the kitchen.

Tim's arms were round Anna from behind as she opened it.

"Always remember that I love you!" he whispered fiercely. "And always will. I'm like my poor father."

"I don't know who I'm like, but I'll always love you, Tim. Did your father never love anyone else?"

"Only as a son and a father. He was a one-woman man. And perhaps he had the same hope I had: that Mother would eventually come back to him. I think if he'd lived longer she might have done."

Anna's hesitation was brief. "She said as much to me this afternoon. When I asked her. Did you never ask her?"

"I wanted to, but I was afraid of her answer. Oh, darling, thank you. I wish he'd known."

"Maybe he did."

When she had fed Whitby and Duffy Anna started rummaging in the fridge.

"What are you doing?"

"Looking for food. I'm ravenous."

"Me too. Bacon and eggs and fried bread?"

When they had eaten they went out into the garden hand in hand. The clouds had stayed away, and the sky was high and so star-studded they had to search among them for the crescent moon. Whitby in the monochrome world was mysterious and undomestic, a black shadow using a clematis as a rope ladder and showing off his kinetic silhouette on the wide top of the old brick wall as he gave himself an all-over double-jointed clean. Their laughter as they watched him rang out in the clear silent air.

"We'll always be glad to get home when we go away," Anna said, as they walked the narrow boundaries and inspected the metamorphosed bushes in their gradations of starlit black and grey.

"I'm glad you said that. I've been wondering . . . Haven't you felt that you'd like to move, Anna? Live out of Town in a more convenient house with bigger rooms and more garden?"

100

"Oh, no, Tim!" The idea dismayed her. "I love Rouge Rue and the way you and your belongings fit it. There's plenty of room, the garden's quite big enough, and it's hardly a long way into the country. Oh, lord . . ."

"What is it?" Tim straightened up from his contemplation of some ghostly golden rod and resumed her hand.

"That was a completely selfish reaction, wasn't it? Perhaps *you* want to move."

"Stick-in-the-mud Le Page? Not on my own account, but if you wanted to it would be different."

"But you'd still feel reluctant?"

"I don't know. I don't think so, if you wanted to go."

"Oh, Tim." It would only ever be his work that made him selfish. "Thank you, but I truly don't want to move and I can't think of anything that would make me feel differently."

Tim wondered whether she was opening the way obliquely to the important subject neither of them had ever broached. But even if she wasn't, the time seemed right.

"Come and sit down. It'll be warm enough for a few minutes." He drew her across to the tree and their long chairs, not yet dew-damp. "Anna," he said when they were settled, "you say you can't think of anything that would make you want to leave Rouge Rue. Does that mean you don't want to have a – another baby, or just that you think you could manage one in this house?"

"Ah." She knew, of course, that this moment had had to come, but as she did not know her own mind on the subject she had decided to let Tim introduce it unless she became aware that it was hanging too uncomfortably tacit between them. That point had not been reached, but it could be that she had just issued him with an invitation. "Tim, I honestly don't know."

"You haven't ruled out the idea, then? I thought you might have done."

"No, I haven't," she said slowly, still not knowing whether this was because her sense of fair play made her feel she should even the score between them, allow him as well as her to be a parent (although her son was dead she did not feel childless), or because she herself wanted another child. His child. "Would you like to be a father, Tim?" What she could see of his face hadn't changed, but a tremor had passed down his long sprawling body. "I want an honest answer."

"I'll try to give you one. I always – saw fatherhood as something that would happen if I got married. Saw it as a natural follow-on. Until I met you, Anna. It's a paradox: you're the only woman I've ever known that I've wanted to marry, yet marriage didn't seem an inevitable step for us. Which seemed to mean that being a father didn't for me. And even now, having achieved the one, I don't any more think of the other as having to follow. Being likely to follow, even."

"Are you saying you'd rather it didn't follow?"

"If it would go against what you want, of course that's what I'm saying." Tim pulled himself upright and leaned forward to take her hand. "And I'll be content. But if you feel . . . If you would like to have another baby, then I'd like it too."

"Oh, Tim." Oh, but she was blessed. He had shown her without knowing it how much he wanted to carry on his line, yet if she refused him he wouldn't sulk or repine, wouldn't take it out on her, let it sour their union. If he didn't let work overtake him sometimes, absorb his attention and blunt his sensitivity, he would probably be too good to be true. "I'm only thirty-five and I'd like another child." She knew what she wanted in the moment of speaking. "So let's try and have one."

Tim shouted "Whoopee!" and pulled her to her feet. Whitby

102

abandoned his toilet and stared at them rigid with surprise, his eyes shining in the starlight and Duffy, who since they left the house had been a mere scuffling in the bushes, pushed his cold wet nose against Tim's leg.

Anna burst out laughing as they hugged one another, pointing from dog to cat. "You struck a chord with the gang, Tim."

"Thirty-five," he whispered. "And I'm thirty-seven. There's plenty of time. D'you want to wait a bit?"

"No."

Picking up a cushion apiece from the chairs, and with no more talk, they went slowly back to the house.

They were lucky: in the morning Anna was able to book a flight to Glasgow at four o'clock the next afternoon, and both the car hire company and the hotel where they had planned to begin their Scottish week were able to accommodate them.

"We can ring the other hostelries when we arrive at the first," Tim said on the telephone, when she had managed to get hold of him. "Or just drive off and hope for the best. We'll get in somewhere."

"We will. And it's time I went to work. I'll go and see Lorna before my afternoon visits."

It was the right sort of corrective to euphoria as well as to anxiety, to carry out successful micro-surgery on a guinea pig and discover that a cat in crisis had turned the corner during the night and was blinking up at her with unclouded eyes as it got to its feet to greet her. By the time Anna found her mother-in-law looking elegant in her armchair she had just about regained her equilibrium, which helped her absorb the sight of Simon lolling on the bed. Before he saw her he was relaxed and smiling, but he got

up the moment he was aware of her and nodded gravely.

"Well?" Lorna demanded. "Have you been on to the airport?"

"Yes. And booked a flight for tomorrow afternoon. And our
hire car and first hotel."

"Oh, that's good. I'm so glad, Anna."

"Thank you." Anna was speaking to Simon as well, who had
brought the other chair round beside Lorna. She sat down, and
with a nod from Lorna, Simon returned to the bed. "You'll be
going back to London tomorrow, Simon?"

Simon glanced at Lorna, who nodded again. "I've decided
to stay till the weekend," he said diffidently, "when hopefully
Lorna'll be well enough to leave with me."

"That's good." Anna thought she meant it, although she
wondered a bit warily how Tim would react to the news
and rejoiced anew that they were going away. "One of the
advantages of being self-employed."

"He should be going tomorrow," Lorna said. "And I've tried
to make him. But he won't leave me."

Anna saw again the look she had seen in Lorna's face when
they were on L'Ancresse Common and she had spoken about
Simon, this time directed openly at its object. And returned, Anna
saw, as she looked from one to the other. Obviously she was
not considered to be the same inhibitory factor as her husband.
Perhaps when they were away she could try to prepare him.

It was another glorious afternoon, and thinking that the dense
holiday crowd which would be milling about the Golden Rose
would render even his tall fairness unremarkable, Simon
decided to risk joining it for a second time, to harden or
dissolve his tentative plans for the coming night. He did not

burden Lorna with them, but he told her of his decision to make another daytime visit, and she saw him off with wary approval.

When he had wandered for a while round the indoor sales area, covertly observing the Charters at stretch and too busy to fix their eyes on anything beyond till, gift wrapping, and the immediate client, Simon took a cold drink to an outside table from where he could still see them. He even ventured to smile at the boy when his mother sent him outside for a break and he stood kicking at the ginger-coloured pebbles that floored the refreshment area.

"You're a hero!" he said, following up the smile. "Why not tell me about the Golden Rose while you take a bit of a rest? It's a super place."

He saw suspicion cloud the pale young face, and was adjudging it an insurmountable reflex reaction when to his pleased surprise Benjamin Charters suddenly returned his smile and shuffled into the other chair at the small table. Perhaps it was that people just didn't bother.

"Yes, it's really nice here," Simon quickly followed up. "Don't you feel lucky, actually living here and being able to help?"

The smile warmed. "You bet! It's jolly hard work, though."

"I can see that. You and your Mum and Dad seem to do it all. You must get awfully tired."

The boy considered. Now, Simon thought, completely off his guard. "S'pose we do. Even though we enjoy it. That's why Mum and Dad are hoping to get some help . . . soon . . ." The boy's tumbling words dropped into silence and his eyes widened as the animation left his face and he stared at Simon. Not afraid of *him*, it seemed to Simon. Just afraid.

"Yes?" Simon encouraged. "You could certainly use some.

People obviously love coming here. Are you interested in the roses?"

"I love them!" The radiance was restored, he had struck lucky.

"You have help with those, I suppose?"

"Gosh, yes. Expert help. I talk to them sometimes and learn how they look after them."

"You'd like to go into the business when you're older?"

"Yes. I like the roses better than – than the people."

"You seem to me to do very well with the people."

The boy shrugged. "Sometimes . . . Grown-up people . . ."

On a pang of pity, Simon wondered if the boy's problems might disappear, or at least lessen, if grown-up people made the effort to draw him out. Emboldened by glances of grim approval being intermittently cast at his table by the boy's parents, he moved the conversation on.

"Is the part of the Golden Rose where you live separate, so that you can get right away when you want to?" Simon waited warily. The boy had no doubt been warned by his parents that the insurance company might try underhand methods. But to his relief the response was open and eager.

"Oh, yes! We live round *there*." Simon was glad, as Benjamin pointed, to see that both parents were occupied with sales. "You can get through to the shop from the inside but where we live is just like anybody's house, you go . . ."

"So you can be absolutely private when you want to," Simon commented provocatively, at the end of a satisfyingly detailed account of the access to the Charters home and its ground floor arrangements.

"Yes, but when I'm writing and so on I like to be . . ." For the second time the face was assailed by fear. "I used to go to the greenhouse that burned," Benjamin finished in a mumble.

106

"I'm so sorry. That was an awful thing to happen. But at least you'll get compensation for the fire from your insurance company. Be able to build another greenhouse. Get more help in the shop."

"Yes!" Suddenly the boy's face shone. "We will!" he went on defiantly. "It'll be great for Mum and Dad!"

It wasn't the reaction Simon had expected, but it was intriguing enough, coupled with his covert study of the boy's parents and the anguished looks they exchanged when they found themselves face to face, to take Simon to a remote part of the garden area. There, strolling along a deserted alley, he rang his temporary employer.

"I'm at the Golden Rose . . . Yes, a great deal of tension . . . Go in tonight? If I can enter without breaking, Mr Taylor. That's trespass enough. I'm sorry . . ." He waited, absently admiring the colourful flowering bushes that lined his path. "No, I'm sorry. But Guernsey's like Britain was fifty years ago and people don't lock doors and windows so there's a chance . . . Yes. Right. I'll talk to you tomorrow."

Back at the Duke of Richmond, Simon banished his coming nocturnal enterprise from his mind while he enjoyed an excellent and leisurely dinner and thought about Lorna and Tim and Anna, trying to suppress the apprehension that always threatened a trio of subjects which should have given him so much pleasure. If things went as he hoped, life in the future would be very good. Tim was the focus of his apprehension; he didn't worry at all about Lorna, of course, and not so much about Tim's new wife, although he had no reason to believe she would help him . . .

"You're a long way away, aren't you, Simon Shaw?"

"I'm sorry? Oh. Hello."

It was the prettiest and most interesting of the girls he had danced with at the wedding, flanked by her parents. Simon, for a good-looking man, was not overly vain, but, unsolicited, she had given him her telephone number and he did wonder, as he took in her provocative but slightly reproachful smile, if she had suggested the Duke of Richmond Hotel for a family dinner outing in the hope that he might still be staying there.

"Mummy, Daddy, this is Simon Shaw from Tim's wedding." Politely, the parents indicated that they remembered. "Awful about his mother, Simon." Tim had warned him that most events, private as well as public, quickly became common knowledge on the island. "How is she?" At least there was no sub-text to the question: his connection with the Le Pages was assumed to be via Tim.

"Getting better," Simon assured her with relief, turning his inward attention to trying to remember the girl's name.

"Deserted tonight, Simon?"

"No. I'm meeting the family at the Princess Elizabeth later." As he lied Simon was aware of a slight inward regret. In ordinary circumstances he would have been happy to see this girl again.

"Come along, Caroline. The waiter's at our table."

It was the father who had obliged him.

"Look, Caroline," he said quietly to the girl. "I'll give you a bell before I leave." With Lorna confined to the hospital and his stay on the island extended, there was no reason, now he thought about it, why he couldn't invite her one evening for a late dinner.

"Great!" Temporarily satisfied with the small victory, the girl turned to her parents. "Lead on, Daddy!"

Looks and smiles from across the restaurant distracted Simon for the rest of his meal from thoughts of what lay immediately ahead, but when he reached his room he began to think solely of his mission. He lay on his bed for a waiting period which seemed interminable. He had not lingered over his coffee as he had intended, afraid of being invited to the girl's table and having his concentration diffused just as he was coming up to the time when he should be honing it. He had learned from experience that he needed all his wits about him on sorties like this, and that he must limber up mentally before take-off.

When he left the hotel he wore a long mac over his sharp black business outline. The night porter nodded, blank-faced, as he went out, and Simon imagined the knowing look he wouldn't be quite able to hide when he returned an hour or so later.

It was a fine, clear night, but he could have wished for cloud. At least the moon was no more than a sliver, but every constellation discovered by man seemed to be in sight from zenith to horizon, and he reduced his nerves a notch by standing in the car-park and picking out the few he knew, led by the Plough.

It was a quarter to two in the morning, and he encountered neither vehicle nor pedestrian on the narrow roads he threaded north. He had studied the terrain the day before, and was able to park in the first of his earmarked possible places: an outer corner of the car-park of a large new hotel a quarter of a mile from the Golden Rose.

Still in the car, he took off the mac and put on the black hood. It had no cover for his face, and he wore it simply to conceal the natural brilliance of his hair, his one feature any witness would recall. After drawing on the close-fitting dark gloves that allowed his fingers most of their dexterity he got out of the car, locked it, and set off at a jog trot – if someone spotted him, it would be better to appear absurd than suspicious.

He had been afraid of his bruises, but to his relief he was scarcely aware of them, and if he had not had a mission he would have enjoyed the sensation of rhythmically moving, aware of his health and strength, the soft cool of the air on his cheeks, the regular thwack of his trainers on the grass verge. He reached the entrance to the Golden Rose sooner than he wished, came to a halt as he looked each way to reassure himself there were no lights other than the lamps illumining the wide gateway, then ran swiftly between them.

The complex was in total darkness, but the starlight showed him there were still a number of cars scattered about the forecourt. Beyond it to the right of the building was public access to the outdoor sales area, and to the left a fence bridged the gap between the peripheral hedge and the building. Behind it was access to the private house, and Simon skirted the left side of the car-park close to the hedge to reach the fence. The gate in it was locked, but it was not yet a trespass to vault it, as he could have reached the other side had he risked crossing the forecourt and going round the back of the sales area.

He landed on gravel with a gritty thud and minimal reaction from his injured shoulder, and froze against the gate, a mercifully dark rectangle in the pale pine of the fence, listening for a sound in response. But there was only the murmur of an owl and the brief shriek of its victim before the silence was restored. Treading cautiously on the crunching pebbles, Simon loped diagonally from the door in the fence to the nearest door to the house, where he froze again. This door, both Benjamin Charters and Anna had told him, led into the kitchen, and beside it was a window, its transom open.

The door was locked, and as he deployed his equipment down through the transom space to give access to the catch on the main window he found himself hoping it would be locked too, that all other windows and all doors would be locked so that he could vault back over the gate and run back to his car and not go where he could never admit to Tim Le Page that he had gone. But when the equipment reached the catch he discovered that the window was merely closed and all that was necessary was to raise the latch and push gently against the glass from inside.

So, fate had bid his trespass go ahead. Simon froze again before climbing over the sill, but the world remained profoundly silent. This time he landed noiselessly on tiles, and pulled the main window to behind him before crossing the kitchen by starlight and passing through its open door into the hall. Here he used his small torch for the first time, turning it on to a staircase and four partly open doors. The first door revealed a large sitting-room, curtains undrawn so that he could see the outlines of the heavy furniture. The second, also with curtains drawn back, contained a sewing machine and an ironing board with iron propped up on it. A kitchen-style cabinet was the only piece of furniture with drawers, and after a few seconds' hesitation he moved on to the third room. Here the curtains were closed, but Simon's torch showed him that it was an office or study with two desks, one a heavy roll-top and the other a large knee-hole.

The roll-top was locked, and Simon turned his attention to the knee-hole. It had four drawers on each side, all of them unlocked, and in the bottom right-hand one he found something that made him draw a sharp breath and take hold of his third piece of equipment, which was round his neck.

He took a couple of photographs, returned the papers carefully to the drawer, and closed it. Then ran towards the faint source of light from the hall.

One moment he was treading lightly and confidently, mission accomplished beyond his most extravagant hopes, the next there was a soft woolly mass between his feet and he was

111

hurtling towards the wood-blocked hall floor, knocking over a small table as he fell and sending whatever it was displaying crashing to the ground.

And the woolly mass was screaming out its shock and fury as it fled up the stairs.

So black cats aren't so lucky. Simon chastised himself for the distracting thought as he leapt back on to his feet, discovered himself to be unhurt, and stood frozen and listening.

"Who's that?"

At least the voice, male, had come from upstairs. But he was unable to unfreeze.

"Is anybody there?"

Now there was the sound of feet, and a sleepy female voice in the distance. Panting with gratitude at finding his mobility restored, Simon fled back to the kitchen and plunged out through the window, retraced his diagonal to the fence and hurled himself over. He hugged the peripheral hedge even more closely than he had hugged it on the way in, and when he had darted through the gates he flung himself into the ditch immediately outside them which he had discovered that morning ran between hedge and verge along the continuation of the lane beyond the Golden Rose. It was so deep the coarse grass almost met over his head, and he decided to stay there until he was sure he was not being pursued, or until a pursuer had passed his hiding-place.

A few minutes went by in a silence broken only by the sounds of hunting and dreaming animals and birds, and a pulse throbbed painfully in his shoulder as the adrenalin drained away. Simon wondered if the Charters were assessing the significance of the break-in, trying to decide whether it was a simple burglary or an attempt to discover more about their greenhouse fire. He had left the papers he had photographed precisely as he had found them, and despite the unlocked desk drawer he was still hopeful his break-in would be interpreted as no more than a search for disposable goods aborted by the family cat. It looked as though Bernard Charters was not coming in pursuit, but he would surely be telephoning the police – Simon thought of Tim with a pang – and his move now must be to put space between himself and the area of the Golden Rose as speedily as possible.

Cautiously he raised his head from the ditch. The lane was clear in both directions, and the only sounds still came from the surrounding fauna. So he pulled himself up on to the verge and began the run back towards his car.

He had scarcely got into his stride when he heard the sound of an engine behind him. The straight stretch of lane beyond the Golden Rose had been empty when he left the ditch, so the vehicle must have come from the nursery. There was no ditch this side of the gates, so all he could do was to shrink back against the hedge. The headlights of the vehicle were raised as he faced it, so dazzling him he was unable to see any details of it, not even how large it was, or how many people were inside it. It seemed to him that it hovered for a lifetime, its dual beam drilling into his eyes until he raised his hands to protect them.

But at last, like an aircraft that has been powerfully motionless while it prepares its engines for take-off, the car hurled itself at the hedge as if it was the start of a runway. Simon saw the silhouette of the driver as it bore down on him, and then saw nothing.

Nine

The afternoon start to their delayed honeymoon meant that Tim and Anna could go into work in the morning. Colleagues in police and practice had urged them to begin their break the evening before, but both found themselves, to their mutual rueful amusement, unable to keep away from their respective work places while there remained a few hours of possible working time.

But they promised to meet at the hospital at noon, and then go home to complete the packing they had begun the night before. There was little left to do: the arrangements for Duffy and Whitby had been reinstated the previous day, and Robin or Clare would collect the dog at two o'clock. Clare rang as Anna was about to follow Tim out of the house, to tell her she had a new lady arriving that afternoon to take up residence at the nursing-home she owned and ran, so that the collector would be husband Robin, whose freelance artistic commitments could be more easily suspended.

"I'm sorry not to see you again before you go, dear one!" Clare purred, in the deep soft tones that so well matched her handsome bulk. "But I'm enchanted you and Tim are on the way at last, and I hope you'll manage not to worry about Tim's mother or anything else while you're in Scotland. I'll go and see Lorna, and take her out if she feels like it, we rather hit it off."

"So I saw. Thank you, Clare. I'm sure she'll be happy to see you."

"*You* sound happy, Anna. There's a note in your voice."

"I am."

Anna stroked her stomach as she hurried out to her car, then tried to ridicule the absurd thought that a new life could be inaugurated to order. It was a glorious morning, the pale diffusion of mature summer sun the sort that warmed the bones without burning the skin. According to the radio it was shining all over the British Isles, and the Glaswegian temperature was expected to reach twenty degrees Celsius by lunchtime.

She was glad, though, Anna realised as she drove down Grange Road and turned into the narrow lane just short of the entrance to the practice, where a deep embrasure in the pavement at the side of the building amounted to a small car-park, to be leaving her adopted home for no more than a week, even though she was taking with her the chief treasure it had yielded.

"Portrait of a workaholic," John Coquelin chided her gently as they met in Reception.

"Can't be, John. I'm late. And I've no list of my own this morning. But I'll help where I can and I'll enjoy handing that cat back to its owner. And thanking everyone for being so accommodating. I'll be away, now, most of next week."

"Anna! Brian thinks you should be away the whole of it."

"He does indeed!" Brian boomed, appearing white-coated from the working area.

"Thanks, but Tim will be going back to work as soon as we get home, so I expect I'll want to. Now, make the most of me, for three hours I'm at everyone's disposal."

Tim had found himself immediately busy on his arrival at the

115

station, and when his mother rang mid-morning to tell him Simon hadn't come to see her as expected, and wasn't at the hotel, he reacted with a sense of irritation he found hard to suppress.

"So what do you expect me to do about it, Mother?"

"Not to snap at me for a start, Tim!"

"I'm sorry. It's just that there's turning out to be a lot of business this morning, and you know I need to finish by noon."

"You shouldn't have gone in this morning. Sometimes you're a little bit too worthy, darling."

"And Anna?"

"And too literal. But I'm worried about Simon. He was talking about going undercover at the Golden Rose."

"So that's probably where he still is." Tim looked out at his tree, a sudden fear making him force the nonchalance which a moment earlier had been a reflex. "Try not to worry, Mother. I'm sure we'll find him there with you when we come to say goodbye." He hesitated. "Were you thinking there was something I could do?"

He heard her sigh. "I was thinking you could help me not to be so worried by telling me not to be so silly. And you've done it. Thank you, darling."

"Oh, Mother . . . I'm sure he'll be all right."

"Yes, Tim. Goodbye."

Still with his eyes fixed on the tree, Tim got up and walked over to the window, his fear growing that Shaw had done a bunk. Fear for his mother, and for himself . . . For himself disappointment, Tim realised in surprise. If Simon Shaw was a phoney and had run out on his mother and her obvious affection for him, he, Tim, would be disappointed in him as well as concerned for his mother. He had been wary of Shaw from the start, and after the attack with the car he had wondered if he was concerned in it, but some part of him had gone on wanting to like the man.

Tim turned from the window with a shrug, telling himself that his mother had to have learned by now to cope with sexual setbacks, and that he knew far too little about Simon Shaw to make any assumptions about him, good or bad, or be affected by what might be the imminent discovery that he was a louse.

The only thing that should be concerning him, Tim told himself with a return of the irritation he somehow found welcome, was the fact that if Shaw had failed to appear by the time he and Anna were due to leave Guernsey their second attempt at a honeymoon would be flawed even if it managed to go ahead: worrying about his mother, neither of them could be the carefree and mutually absorbed couple a honeymoon should engender.

He was grateful for the arrival of his Sergeant Mahy, to fill him in about the morning's unprecedented discovery by an early morning patrol: a dead body carrying no means of identification.

"Sit down, Ted, and tell me about it. Another cup for the sergeant, please," he asked the constable arriving with a pot of coffee, relieved to find his irritation turning into amusement: his usual single cup had been upgraded, no doubt as a delicate send-off gesture. "All I've heard so far is that it's a male with not a single clue on him as to his identity."

"Not a single clue that can help here and now, Tim. There's a couple of labels in his clothes: three M and S and another no one here recognises. Scope there for longer-term investigation, of course. Forensics have hardly started, but there's a camera on a cord round the neck. Open, with no film in it. I didn't need to be told that his chest and stomach had been mashed into a hedge."

"So you've seen him?" *Another hit-and-run.* Tim found himself suddenly out of breath.

"Yes. I'm afraid it's one I'll remember." DS Mahy took a gulp of coffee, as Tim noted absently that his usual ruddy complexion was comparatively pale.

"Ted . . ." He wanted to walk over to the window, get closer to his tree, but he didn't think his legs would carry him and he remained in his chair. "Was he young?"

"Yes. Lean and fit, too. Crying shame. That anyone . . ."

"Yes. Ted . . ."

"You all right, Tim?"

"I'm not sure. Did he . . . Was he very fair?"

Ted stared, putting his coffee cup back on its saucer without drinking. "He was. How d'you—"

"Was he close to the Golden Rose?"

DS Mahy considered. "Route de Glycine . . . Yes, he must have been. My God, Tim, d'you—"

"I know who it is, yes." Tim got up then, steadying himself against his desk. "Take me to the mortuary, will you, Ted? Now, this minute."

"But sir . . ."

"Now."

"The post-mortem may have started," Ted said warily, as he turned into the hospital grounds. "But you can still—"

"Wherever he is, I have to see him."

To his absurd sensation of relief, the body was still in its cold box. Before the sheet was drawn back Tim had no doubt whose face he would see. But the shock of confirmation was still so intense that for a moment his head swam and he let his strong stocky sergeant take his weight.

"Sir . . ." The sergeant put an arm round Tim's shoulders.

"Don't you recognise him, Ted?" Tim asked dreamily. "Don't you recognise Simon Shaw? You met him at my wedding."

"Yes . . . Dear God, Tim, I can see now. But he doesn't—"

"Look like himself. No." Tim leaned forward and closed the blue eyes, staring in astonishment at the ceiling striplight. Simon hadn't had much colour but he had been tanned, and the pallor now of his skin transformed the handsome face which death had already diminished. But the face was undamaged, and Tim was shudderingly thankful that the sheet still covered the body below the shoulders.

"This is the body of Simon Shaw, a visitor from London. I'll let you have particulars," he told the attendant correctly before turning away with his sergeant's support, and staggering like a drunk along the corridor.

Ted pushed him into a wayside chair, but Tim immediately struggled back to his feet. "My mother . . . I have to go and tell her. Be my crutch to the Victoria wing, Ted, and then go and ring the airport and tell them Anna and I won't be on the four o'clock plane to Glasgow. Oh, God, make it a men's room first."

He managed to get to one before being sick. After that, and a few minutes on the lavatory seat with his head between his knees, he was able to walk through the hospital unassisted.

It felt like the hardest thing he had ever had to do. So hard, he was desperately hoping that Anna had arrived so that he could tell her first, and secure her back-up for when he told his mother. When they reached the Vic wing he asked Reception to ring his mother's room and, if his wife was there, call her out on a piece of business.

She was there. When she saw his face she crouched in front of the chair where Ted had put him.

"Oh, God, Tim, what is it?"

119

"It's Simon. His body was found this morning. Crushed into the hedge outside the Golden Rose. A car again."

What he couldn't understand was his own sense of grief, almost as strong as his terror of what the news would do to his mother. Grief for the waste of a young, healthy life was natural, but what he was feeling was more than that, it was grief for Simon Shaw.

"I've asked Ted to cancel our flight. I'm sorry I didn't ask you first, darling, but it seemed—"

"Of course. I'll cancel everything else after . . . Oh, Tim, how are we going to do it?"

"By telling her. Straight out. That's how *I'd* prefer it. No gradual realisation, ghastly slow sinking in. Tell her, and then be there."

"Yes. Oh, you're right. Come on. She was anxious when I left, afraid something had happened to prevent our departure."

"I'll leave you now then, sir."

"Yes, Ted. Thank you." Tim could see in his sergeant's face relief at the presence of Anna. "I'll never forget how you've helped me today. I'll see you later, I want to be at the centre of this particular investigation."

"Could someone cancel the chits and tickets in here, please, Ted?" Anna held out the travel folder already tucked into the large bag she had been going to take to Scotland. DS Mahy took it silently, with a nod, and walked quickly away after an anxious glance at Tim.

His mother was in her chair but straining towards the door, her face tight with anxiety. Even when she saw them it scarcely relaxed, to Tim's relief. At least she was on the way to the truth.

"Darling, thank goodness! So what was all that about, Anna? Tim, Simon still hasn't appeared, and now the Duke tell me his bed wasn't slept in. I'm sure something terrible has happened to him!"

If only she was! But she had given him his start. "It has, Mother." He went and knelt at her feet, taking her hand. "Simon was found dead early this morning. He'd been hit by a car in the lane outside the Golden Rose."

For a moment she sat still, staring at him, her face expressionless. Then, it seemed to Tim in slow motion, it contorted, the eyes widening, the upper lip arching, the nostrils flaring. As the lower lip dropped there came from the widening mouth a scream so grievously piercing Tim had to restrain his hand from clamping across the ear-splitting void.

After a lifetime the scream subsided to a moan, and his mother took her hand from his and fastened her arms across her chest before starting to sway backwards and forwards.

"Lorna. Hush, Lorna." Anna was round the back of the chair, fondling Lorna's shoulders, pressing her cheek into Lorna's hair. "He wouldn't want this."

"He would, he would." It was a mumble, but that was what Tim thought she had said.

"No," he told her. "No one would." He twisted up towards the hovering nurse, seeing vaguely that the doorway seemed to be crowded with other members of the hospital staff. "Bring a doctor, will you?"

When a doctor arrived a minute or so later, Lorna was still swaying and keening. He put a needle into her unresisting arm, and ordered her transfer to her bed.

"I hope it won't put her out completely," Tim murmured to him when she was resettled, stroking her forehead as her head thrashed from side to side. "If it does, when she wakes it'll be worse for her than ever."

"It's only a strong sedative. She's gone into shock, that's

why she isn't trying to deny what you've told her, ask you any questions. When she comes out of it she'll panic and shouldn't be alone. Can you stay with her?"

"Of course."

They both stayed, one each side of the bed, and at the end of an hour Lorna appeared to relax. But almost instantly she shot upright, grabbing a hand of each of them and turning from one to the other with a desperate face.

"Tim! For God's sake tell me it isn't true! Not Simon!"

"It is true, Mother. Simon was run down by a car in the night, in the lane outside the Golden Rose. He would have died instantly. He wouldn't have suffered."

"But he shouldn't have died at all. Not *Simon*. Oh, God, how could you have let that happen? How could you?"

To the enormous relief of both Tim and Anna, Lorna burst into a storm of weeping. She wept for a long time, the bed shaking with the force of her grief. The violence of her reaction to the news of Shaw's death had frightened Tim as well as amazed him, but his fear subsided with her weeping, and he found his irritation coming back. What had happened to his mother's native stoicism? She had had numberless encounters over the years with men of all ages and conditions – he had always reluctantly known that he had seen no more than the tip of the iceberg – so how could she be so devastated, in her sixth decade, by the death of a toyboy? He felt ashamed for her. And of her, he realised, then was ashamed of himself for the reaction even while wishing that the hospital staff could be kept in ignorance of what had so shattered their patient.

But that was hardly possible. Other members of the police force would soon be at her bedside, not to hold her hand but to question her about her boyfriend's state of mind, what he had said, what his intentions for the previous evening had been and so on and so on . . . In one flash, Tim saw the whole dreary stretch of the investigation in front of them, a long dry road bordered by desert.

"I want to see him," Lorna said, when the weeping had subsided to huge intermittent sobs that shook her whole body.

"Mother, I don't think—"

"I have to see him."

"I'll go with her," Anna said. Partly because she found herself not wanting to be the only member of their trio who had not seen Simon Shaw in death, and partly because once was enough for Tim. "It isn't far, Lorna," she whispered into the tousled hair. "The mortuary's here in the hospital."

"So I'm near him . . ."

"Come on, Mother, then, if you insist." It was starting to be difficult not to let the irritation show.

Together they helped Lorna out of bed and into her dressing-gown. When it was fastened she pulled herself from their grasp, picked up a comb and walked unaided to a looking-glass. "But he won't see me, it doesn't matter," she murmured, when she had pulled it a few times through her untidy hair, and was sagging when Tim reached her. Anna went out into the corridor and asked for a wheelchair. Then, when they had manoeuvred Lorna into it, managed – more easily, he hoped, than she suspected – to dissuade Tim from accompanying them.

"I'll go in alone," Lorna told her, as they arrived.

Someone from the Victoria wing had rung through, and the body was ready. Lorna got out of the chair outside the room where it was lying, waving away assistance, and Anna waited with racing heart for another cry to pierce the walls. But there was silence, which continued as Lorna came out with the young man who had taken her in and who she allowed to help her back into her chair. Then she looked up at Anna, her eyes so grieved Anna had to turn away.

"D'you want to see him?" the young man asked her.

"Yes."

It was a relief that the body didn't look like Simon Shaw, like any living being, but before she could turn away she had superimposed on the still flesh the animation of its life. As she had done with Mickey, when she had looked into the unseeing eyes of her eleven-year-old son.

"Are you all right?"

Anna nodded, unable to speak, and was escorted out to Lorna. They made the return journey in silence.

Tim was talking to some nurses outside Lorna's room. It was the look of Anna, now, which alarmed him the more, and when they had helped Lorna back on to the bed and were sitting as before each side of her, he asked his wife if she was all right.

"I will be. It made me remember Mickey."

"Oh, God." Tim smote his forehead. "I should have thought!"

"I'd still have gone. It had to come. Mickey was my son, Lorna," she said, although Lorna wasn't looking a question, she was staring into space. It just might help her start to regain a sense of proportion if she thought about her daughter-in-law having lost a son. "He was eleven and he was . . ."

Anna stopped, looking across at Tim. Only then realising the significance at that moment of how Mickey had died.

"Anna's son was run down by a car, Mother," he said, so clearly and firmly that he caught her attention.

"What did you say, Tim?" she asked slowly, turning her head towards him.

"I said that Anna's son Mickey was killed by a car. He was eleven. She'll never get over it but she's learned to live with it."

Lorna turned her head the other way. "Well done, Anna!" she said, with a ghastly sprightliness which had both her son and her daughter-in-law involuntarily recoiling. "Well done! I wonder if *I'll* ever manage that?" And she went off into a paroxysm of hysterical laughter.

The laughter was shorter-lived than the earlier weeping, and when it was dying down Tim, feeling self-righteous as well as indignant, told Lorna he would never have thought to hear her comparing the death of a son with the death of a toyboy.

"For heaven's sake, Mother, try and pull yourself together! Anna lost her *son*, and you're behaving as if the world has come to an end because your *boyfriend*'s dead! A boyfriend young enough to be *your* son!"

"Oh, Tim." Lorna wiped her eyes, then picked up his hand. "Simon *is* my son. And your brother."

Ten

Watching Tim's face, Anna found herself remembering the first time she had met him, her neighbour at a dinner table, because it was the only other time when he had looked totally unfamiliar.

He had shuddered as Lorna spoke, and then his face had settled into a sort of grave attentiveness. The face of a policeman at work.

"Does anyone else in Guernsey know this, Mother?"

"In Guernsey? No one."

"Good. We'll leave it that way during the investigation, I'll have more clout if no one knows that I—" Another shudder, making Anna hope he was coming back to life. But the terrible composure was immediately restored. "We'll say he was an old friend of the family."

But Simon Shaw was his brother, Tim raged, Simon Shaw had been far more deeply inside his mother than his wildest nightmares had imagined, as deeply as he had been himself. His brother, the dear younger brother he had always longed for, who had stood within reach of his caress and looked at him with what he now knew had been a tremulous hope that he might soon be accepted and loved.

But soon was too late.

Savagely Tim pushed the anguish away from him, tried to push away every emotion save his rage. There would be time for grief later, when he had brought whoever had murdered his brother to justice. Now, he dare not attempt to absorb his loss because the process would show, he must force himself to be as inwardly detached as he would appear on the surface. Shock was making that easy now, but when it wore off he would have to spend every waking moment at work on it. And the price he was going to pay was detachment from everyone and everything which a few moments ago had made up his life. Even his wife, who seemed suddenly a long way away. He would have to hope she had the understanding to see that even with the two people he was closest to he must be as he would be among his colleagues and the public if he was to hold his role as prosecutor.

"I must go. See my Chief and get things under way. He let me head the investigation when my cousin Charles was murdered, so there shouldn't be any trouble with the death of – a friend." Tim shuddered again.

"Of course, darling," Lorna whispered.

Now he had to force himself to focus his eyes on his mother. "I'm sorry I said what I did," he told her. "But I didn't know."

"Of course you didn't, Tim."

"Why didn't you tell me earlier? Years and years earlier?" He didn't know, either, that he was going to say that. And so angrily.

"Simon was adopted by Gina. She'd lost a baby and was in a bad way. I'd lost Geoffrey, he died before Simon was born. He wouldn't have let Simon go, but he wasn't there and I'd learned I was no good as a mother."

The old Tim, Anna thought fearfully, would have offered some kindly gesture of dissent, but the new one continued to stand frowning, tapping a foot as he waited impatiently for more information.

Lorna showed no awareness of the change. "No one in Guernsey knew I was pregnant when Geoffrey and I left, and no one in England except Gina and our lawyers knew Simon was my son. I saw a lot of him as he grew up, because I saw a lot of Gina. Gina had told him he was adopted as soon as he was old enough to understand, and when he was thirty and completely independent of our generation she told me she wanted him to know that I was his blood mother. It's only a couple of months since his birthday, so we were still excited by each other and I can see how you were afraid—"

"So why didn't you tell me when you arrived? At least I could have . . ." But he mustn't speak, or even think, about what he could have done.

"Tim!" The sudden severity in Lorna's voice caught his attention, and the long focus of his eyes shortened to take her in.

"Well?

"It was your wedding! I know I've done some upstaging in my time, but I wouldn't upstage your wedding. Simon and I agreed on that. I could see you were upset when I said I'd hang on in Guernsey until Simon had finished his assignment then leave with him before you got home, but we were going to come back together in a week or so after your return and tell you then."

"I see. All right." He couldn't think, now, about what might have been. "Mother, I need to know all there is to know about Simon's assignment." Anna noted with a pang that despite his self-control Tim was no longer calling his brother by his surname. "Seeing that he was run down outside the Golden Rose. How did he get it?"

"He got it because the MD of the insurance company investigating the possibility of fraud is Gina's brother, which makes him Simon's adoptive uncle. But he got it on merit too, he's done some good work in the City. Tim!" For the second time the imperious note in his mother's voice had Tim coming temporarily to attention. "Constance could have followed him last night. Waited until he came out of the Golden Rose, and then—"

"You said no one in Guernsey knew he was your son," Tim said sharply.

"No one does. But if she'd got the idea he was important to me in a different way . . . The way *you* thought."

The way he knew Constance Lorimer thought, too, from what she had said when he had visited her. But he wouldn't tell his mother that. "Even then, she'd have to have been shadowing him round the clock to know he'd be going out in the middle of the night. Which isn't very likely."

"I suppose not," Lorna agreed reluctantly, then let out a cry that had Anna and Tim shying like nervous racehorses. "Gina! I have to tell her. Oh, God. Anna . . ."

"I'll stay with you. No one's expecting me anywhere else. Tim, you go!"

He went willingly and without a word, because there was nothing helpful he could say or do. When he had gone Anna asked Lorna if she would like her to make the call. Lorna's face looked lopsided, as if she had had a stroke, and everything about her seemed smaller.

"Yes, but I must do it myself. Don't go far away, though. I'll want you afterwards."

Anna left the building and strolled about in the sunshine, shivering in the warm air and worrying about Tim. It was only as she looked at her watch and decided it was time to be back that she remembered she was on her honeymoon and gave a snort of overwrought laughter.

She found Lorna in tears, but calmer.

"Is she coming over?"

"No. And I got the feeling she'll never come. That she couldn't." The way Anna couldn't go to the place where Mickey had died. "We didn't get round to talking about the funeral, but Tim told me we'll have to wait a while, till they release Simon's body. I'm glad Gina isn't coming, I don't think we could take each other just now. Anna, what am I going to do about all the days and weeks and months ahead?"

"You're not going to think about them." Anna took one of the suddenly agitating hands. "Lorna, any advice I give you . . . I've lived through it."

"I'd forgotten!" Lorna stared at her, shocked. "I know I'm self-obsessed, but to forget that! Forgive me."

"There's nothing to forgive. Except for a few saints grief is a selfish emotion, and you have to give in to it to get through it. For a long time my dead son and I were the only two people in the world." Anna thought with a pang of one of the saints, her then husband Jimmy, patiently sublimating his own grief into unwearying effort to help her through hers.

"Oh, Anna. I know already what you mean. I've lost Simon, but thank heaven I've found *you*. But I'm not going to cling to you. Or to Tim." To her pleased surprise, Anna saw the fleeting suggestion of a smile. "Now, having said that, may I leave this hospital and come to Rouge Rue?"

Tim's anger needed as much fuel as he could give it, and as he drove into Town he was glad to find it engulfing his mother as well as fate and Constance Lorimer and the Charters. His brother was – had been – thirty years old, and she had only just told him he was her son. Deference to the anger-inducing Gina, he supposed, but it had meant three wasted decades, above all for himself and Simon, who had been denied their rightful contact. His mother had known Simon was her second son and had been able to enjoy his company, but he, Tim, had been deprived of his only sibling. "Selfish bitch!" he hissed aloud, as he slewed too quickly into his parking place in the police courtyard.

When he had switched off he sat a few seconds to recover his new facade, approving his closed face in his rear mirror before getting out. When he reached his office he looked out angrily at the tree and turned his blind against the sun before ringing for Ted.

"I want an immediate incident room set up. Whatever authority the Chief gives me, we need that. I thought the conference room, there isn't anything on the horizon needing it and even if there were—"

"It's under way, sir. In the conference room. The Chief asked to see you the moment you got in."

"Thanks, Ted." His sergeant was looking at him with concern, he'd have to say something more. And temper his stoicism with Ted as well as with his mother and his wife: to appear more detached than was his wont could excite as much speculation as letting his sorrow show. Fortunately he hadn't shared his doubts about Simon with any of his colleagues. Because from the start he hadn't wanted them to be true, Tim realised with a fresh pang that had him catching his breath. "Don't look so worried," he managed, aware of his lips stretching in a reflex smile, a gesture that already felt unfamiliar. "But you're right, Ted, I *am* upset. Simon Shaw was a very old friend."

"Oh, Tim! I hadn't realised. I thought your shock was for your mother."

"It is, she and Simon's mother are old friends as well, and

she has to tell her. But it's my shock too. That's why I'm so keen to lead the investigation."

"So perhaps that's why when you see the Chief you should play down your personal involvement."

"I couldn't play down my personal involvement when my cousin Charles was murdered last year, Ted. And the Chief gave me the investigation. But you're right, of course, no need to say anything now beyond that the victim was a friend of the family." Tim paused, to make his next announcement as dramatically distracting as possible. "And that he came to Guernsey on a hush-hush assignment."

"*What!*"

As he had hoped, he had pushed himself out of Ted's picture of the murdered man. "You heard me, Ted."

"You knew this, sir?"

"Yes. It's to do with the fire at the Golden Rose. Simon . . . Shaw runs – ran – a detective agency in London." He had to pause and cough, to disguise the fact that he was suddenly out of breath again. "And he was here on behalf of the insurance company the Charters are insured with. The local branch got in touch with their head office in London because of not being entirely satisfied that the fire was as accidental as the owners claimed it to be, given the presence in the burned greenhouse of those valuable pictures. Doubt had been expressed recently about their value – and then they went up in smoke. Shaw was undercover, but he told me because of – of our old friendship, and because he thought that as a policeman I might be able to offer some local input." He had to pause, to put aside the sudden vivid picture of Simon's eyes as they pleaded with him to visit the Golden Rose unofficially. He hadn't done it, and now that Simon was dead he never could. "He hadn't uncovered anything criminal so there was no action for me to take. Perhaps last night he did." And perhaps last night he himself had broken the law . . . Tim got to his feet to hide another shudder. "I should be telling this to the Chief, Ted. And whether or not I head the investigation, I should be authorising the closing and cordoning off of the Golden Rose, and a uniform in the house. Will you see to it?"

The Chief, too, was riveted by Tim's revelation of why the murdered man had come to Guernsey.

"That must be the reason he was carrying nothing to identify him," he said, as he strolled to his window and looked out on his slightly different view of the tree. Tim wondered idly if he, too, took strength from it. "I'm grateful for the short cut, Tim, and of course I want you to head the investigation on the ground." The Chief turned from the window and surveyed him with mild concentration. "If you're certain your judgment won't be clouded by your family's friendship with the victim. You handled your cousin's murder very well, but friendship can generate as much feeling as family and if you think—"

"I can handle it, sir." Tim thought his Chief had been obliquely and delicately stating his knowledge that Tim had not had strong personal feelings for his murdered cousin. "Simon and I only met on family holidays so it isn't as if I've lost someone I was close to." A truth and a lie in one. At least the lie was the worst he would have to tell about his brother.

"Um. All right." The Chief came back to his desk and sat down. "There's a lot to be looked into, legwork to be apportioned, you'd better get to it."

"Thank you, sir." Tim hesitated. "I've just issued instructions for the Golden Rose to be closed and cordoned off, and a uniform in the house. With my knowledge of Shaw's mission I knew that whoever was to head the investigation would want—"

"Of course, Tim. With your knowledge you could have done it sooner." *Should have done it sooner.* The Chief was telling him what he knew: that he should have charged Ted with the task immediately he had identified Simon's body. And he hadn't even had the excuse, then, of knowing who Simon was. "Anything else at this stage?"

"I don't think so, sir." He could mention the outside possibility of the murder having something to do with the first hit-and-run. But if he did he would turn the spotlight he had just deflected from himself onto Simon *vis-à-vis* their mother and that would be dangerous and difficult. Unless, of course, the first attack had been aimed at Simon too, and their mother had simply been in the way. Which would mean that Constance Lorimer was innocent . . .

"Two car nasties for you, Tim, within a week, both involving people close to you. I'm sorry. D'you see any possibility of a connection?"

He was glad to have the decision made for him. "Both Shaw and my mother were convinced the car in L'Hyvreuse was aiming at her, sir. And it was she who was hit. And although as you know there's no forensic evidence pointing to Constance Lorimer's car being involved, there *is* bad blood between her and my mother. As you know, too, I've been favouring Mrs Lorimer for that first hit-and-run, but I feel it's unlikely she could have been responsible for the second." He wouldn't tell the Chief, or any of his colleagues, that Constance Lorimer believed the dead man to have been his mother's lover. "But of course there has to be the possibility of a connection via Shaw, even though I see no way the Charters could have known about his assignment before last night, when he could have been spotted in or near their property. He visited the Golden Rose as a tourist, but that was after the attack on my mother so it isn't significant so far as the first hit-and-run is concerned. I'm inclined to think the two attacks are unconnected, sir. A scientist friend once told me that coincidence in real life, as opposed to fiction, is more likely than not."

"So there's a lot of work to do, Tim. Get your troops together and tell them what you've just told me."

Eleven

It didn't seem necessary to deploy a large force. Tim sent a couple of uniforms to the Duke of Richmond to try to find out when Simon had left the hotel, if he had said anything on departure, if he had been alone, and if he had taken his hire car. Should the car be missing from the small car-park carved out of the corner of Cambridge Park opposite the hotel, another uniform was to get its particulars from the car hire company – DS Mahy would give details – and seek it in an outward sweep from the Golden Rose. He himself, with DS Mahy and back-up, would look for it in the nursery grounds, in the course of interviewing the Charters.

He did not tell his team that he himself would later in the day have another word with Constance Lorimer. Alone, because he did not want even Ted to suspect a special relationship – the wrong one or the right one – between his mother and Simon. If he brought Ted in, or any other member of the force, that would become an inevitable factor in the investigation. Calling on her alone would mean, of course, that his second questioning of her had to be unofficial, but for the moment that would suit him.

Since the discovery of Simon's body, forensic experts had been at work on the area of hedge and roadway where he had been found. Tim had them contacted and asked to remain *in situ* until he arrived, then be ready to follow him to the Charters' home quarters to examine the family cars and vans and look for evidence in and out of the house to indicate that Simon had been there. The fact that Bernard Charters had telephoned the station to ask for the detective inspector suggested to Tim that he had.

Rain, still thinly falling, had come sudden and heavy in the early morning, and despite his resolute professionalism Tim was unable to see it trickling down the windscreen without equating it with tears. The sky was low, grey and featureless, and his outer world was as different as his inner from its brilliant yesterday. Even the lane outside the Golden Rose, which had been so beguiling a lead into the popular small complex, looked tired and dreary, the hedgerow greens which in spring had been so bright and variegated now a uniform sage colour where they were not brown with the mud from passing motorists and the attentions of the forensic team.

The place where Simon had died was a small crushed embrasure in a stretch of hawthorn above a churning of grass and soil.

"Morning, Tim." It was the female senior pathologist who came over to the car when it stopped short of the wide gateway and Tim wound his window down. The rain had scarcely affected her wealth of teased blonde hair and her good looks were adorned as at all times with a great deal of make-up, but Tim, who had taken her to a couple of police dos before he met Anna, knew that her skill and intelligence were formidable. He could have let her body block his view of the death spot, but a force stronger than his will compelled him to look beyond her for traces of Simon's body and feel sick with relief that none was evident.

"Morning, Doreen. Anything turned up?"

"Nothing."

"Not even tyre marks?"

137

"He was hit before the rain came, when the verge would have been rock hard. Now it's a swamp, and even without the rain the area would probably have been too grassy. Coarse, thick stuff. But if the vehicle involved belongs to the Golden Rose, it'll have collected the local soil and flora on its tyres anyway. We'll follow you up to the house."

"Go through the sales area and turn left." Tim hesitated. "You all right these days?"

"Never better." The pathologist hesitated in her turn. "Congratulations, Tim, but I'm sorry about the honeymoon."

"Third time'll be lucky. See you in a minute."

A uniform released the police barrier across the entrance to the Golden Rose and Tim drove on to the forecourt. A notice on a pole had been stuck into the earth at the front edge regretting closure until further notice. The area behind the building was deserted, but Bernard Charters was standing under the porch outside his back door and came forward as Tim got out of the car. Another uniform remained in the open doorway behind him.

Tim gave Charters good morning, noting the tension in the face visible even through the merging moustache and beard. But it was showing in the rest of him too as he stood lacing his hands and moving from foot to foot.

"I asked for you, Inspector Le Page," he said at once. "When the police told me just now what had happened, I asked for you. Someone broke into my house last night." It was only as he heard the accusation that Tim realised how much he had been hoping not to hear it. "I suppose it must have been the man found dead in the lane, but I didn't kill him." Bernard Charters spoke as though he was repeating a statement he had memorised. "I was in bed when I heard him downstairs. I thought of running after him, but I was in my pyjamas and anyway while I was wondering what to do I heard a car start up. But I'm told the dead man was on foot. I can't understand—"

"We'll get to that," Tim interrupted lightly. If Bernard Charters wasn't genuinely bewildered, he was a very good actor. "Now, I'm afraid I must ask you to allow a couple of pathologists into your house, to confirm that somebody did break in, and what he was about while he was inside. I have a warrant, Mr Charters."

"Of course you have. And as you can see, your forces are already in occupation without one." Tim had the absurd feeling that the man's only alternative to his flow of talk would have been total silence. "When I told your PC Lainé that the intruder hadn't been upstairs he confined my wife, my son and myself to the first floor pending your arrival, but then heeded my plea to await you outside."

"Sir . . ." PC Lainé shuffled his feet uneasily.

"You were entirely in order, Constable," Tim reassured him. "And you can go now and help with the examination of the parked cars and the grounds."

The constable retreated with a relieved smile, passing Dr Roberts and her junior colleague as they appeared round the corner of the building.

"Come in, all of you." Charters made an outsize gesture towards the kitchen window. "You can see how he got in and out. As you know, Mr Le Page, people in Guernsey don't lock their windows at night. My wife and I have been assimilated to that extent." His tone was sardonic. "Before that he probably vaulted the gate, which we do keep locked. Otherwise he'd have to have gone all the way round the building."

The four further intruders murmured their thanks as they filed past him.

"Did you find any evidence of loss or disturbance inside the house?" Tim asked, advancing into the hall as the pathologists began examing the kitchen window.

He was aware of Charters' deep-set eyes moving quickly from side to side as if reflecting their owner's sensation of being caged. "No loss, Inspector." But Charters' arm had swung out towards the open doorway of what was clearly an office as if attempting to protect its contents, and Tim thought of the empty camera round Simon's neck. It was a professional reflex, but it stayed with him as a personal pain, and for an anguishing moment he wondered if he would have the strength to lead the investigation to its conclusion. "As for disturbance . . . The man knocked over this small table and the vase on it shattered. Your clever pathologists may be able to find fresh scratches on the floor and the table, and the remains of the vase are in the bin. He must have fallen over the cat, it came howling upstairs. I'd already been wakened by the noise of the table and the vase, and I shouted out. Of course when I got downstairs he'd disappeared. I stood where we're standing now, thinking about giving chase. Thinking, as I told you, that I wasn't wearing so much as a dressing-gown. And then I heard a car engine start up, and decided it would be a waste of time."

"And a waste of time to ring the police?" Tim demanded sternly.

Bernard Charters shrugged. "Nothing appeared to have been taken, and I was convinced, as I still am, that the intruder was a detective hired by the insurance company I'm claiming on for my greenhouse. I didn't know insurance companies were above the law, Inspector."

"When they employ detectives they can't dictate their methods." It was Ted who said it while Tim winced. "Now, the detective inspector and I would like to have a look at your office."

"Of course, Inspector." Charters offered what Tim had begun to think was his habitual ironic smile, and indicated the open doorway. Tim and his DS followed him through it and stood looking round the tidy, business-like room.

"Your desks are kept locked?" Ted Mahy asked.

"The roll-top is, my business records are in it. It wasn't tampered with. The knee-hole . . ." Charters shrugged again, and Tim felt a stab of excitement as the nonchalant pose struck him as a little too elaborate. "Just family things – photos, Benjamin's school reports and so on. Nothing to lock up there. Feel free to look through everything, Mr Le Page. Well, you will of course, whether I invite you to or not." Bernard Charters walked across to the roll-top desk and unlocked it with a key taken from the long central drawer of the knee-hole. Then he turned and looked intently at Tim. "Again, Inspector, neither my wife nor I, nor our son of course, so much as set eyes on the man you found dead in the ditch. I didn't take a vehicle out, anyway, after five o'clock yesterday evening. But of course you'll find the local soil and flora on all our wheels. These lanes are narrow, and you have to pull close into the side when you meet a car coming."

"I appreciate that, Mr Charters." But not the fact that the rain had come at the wrong time. The tyres would be dry and dusty whether or not a member of the family had murdered Simon. "Now, you talked about an insurance company. You believe the break-in was connected with your recent fire?"

"I'm convinced of it. They've been hedging on my claim because of the valuable pictures that were destroyed with the greenhouse. Since last night I've seen that as playing for time while their undercover agent went to work." Another pause. "He must have died disappointed, Mr Le Page. I have nothing to hide."

"We'll be talking about that, Mr Charters. Now, if you'll excuse me for a moment." Doreen was hovering, and he accompanied her back to the kitchen.

"No fingerprints, Tim, but we weren't expecting any. If the break-in was ordered by the insurance company they'd hardly have appointed an amateur."

"Doreen . . ." He had to ask. "*Was* it a break in?"

She was looking at him in surprise. "I suppose not, sir, strictly speaking. Nothing was broken and no lock was forced."

He was comforted. "You'd better try the study. After you've collected any clothes you feel could be significant. Don, perhaps you'll get out to the vehicles."

When he came back into the hall, Bernard Charters had his eyes raised to the staircase as if in appeal. His wife and son were on their way down. The wife had her hand on the boy's shoulder, and both faces were wide eyed and grave.

"Good morning, Mrs Charters, Benjamin." Tim still spoke lightly, in a social tone. "I was just about to ask your husband if he'll be good enough to come with me to the station where we can more easily get down to a helpful chat. I hope you're going to be able to help me, sir," he went on, turning to the house-holder with a false smile. Normally he hated these moments, when he must strike fear into the hearts of people who might be innocent, but this morning he was delighted to be issuing the usual invitation. Bernard Charters might be innocent, but if he wasn't, if he had murdered Simon, there would be nothing too bad for him, and the sooner he started to taste fear . . .

". . . just get a jacket."

Savagely Tim wrenched his thoughts back to the professional. His sudden personal rage had made him miss Charters' reaction to the invitation. He must never let up on his self-policing.

DS Mahy was speaking.

"One other thing, sir, before we go. Dr Roberts and her colleague will need to take away the clothes you were wearing at the time of the break-in last night, plus any clothes you could have put on if you'd gone outside. You've told us you didn't follow the dead man out into the lane, but I'm afraid that in murder inquiries, as I'm sure you'll appreciate, we can't take anyone's word for granted."

"Any suspect's word. Yes, of course I appreciate that."

"Anyone, innocent or guilty, who was close to the scene of the crime," DS Mahy amended, and Tim gave him a swift grateful smile "So if you'll be good enough to indicate . . ." He stopped speaking as the boy began to cry, shuddering against his mother's side.

"It's just routine," Tim took up, having to force himself to sound soothing. "And covered by the search warrant. Has anything been washed this morning?"

"No! Nor last night, Inspector!" Charters' suddenly sharp tone was a shock, after his hitherto quiet responses. "As I've told you, and will continue to tell you, I have nothing to hide. You'd better ask your colleague," he went on, turning to Doreen. "Seeing that I'm going to have to undress."

"I'll send him in," Tim said. "And see you outside when you're ready, sir. Wait in the house, will you, Sergeant? I'll be having a look round outside." He hesitated. "You've finished in the lane, Dr Roberts?"

Doreen nodded. "All done and dusted, Inspector. Your timing was perfect."

"Thank you." He was acting correctly, but it coincided with his sudden intense desire to retrace his brother's last footsteps. When he had sent Doreen's sidekick inside he went slowly across to the gate in the fence shutting off the forecourt and stood staring up at it. Quite a height, with a foot or so of fence on top. He was fit enough to have vaulted it too, but he wouldn't choose to, and he wondered with another awful pang if Simon had felt the injuries he had sustained in L'Hyvreuse. The key was in the lock on the inside and he turned it and went through, walking close to the leafy boundary along which Simon would have loped. His heart was beating so strongly by the time he reached the gate he was glad of the excuse to pause a moment for a word with the constable on duty.

"A shocking business, sir."

"It is indeed, Constable."

"Not like Guernsey, sir."

"Not a bit like Guernsey, no."

"Someone from the mainland, of course, sir. Not a Guern."

"No. Well, carry on."

"Thank you, sir."

Tim thought the idiotic exchange had been a slight help. His heartbeat had subsided, and he had gathered his courage for a closer look at the place where his brother had died.

The pathologists had done their work, so he didn't have to tread warily. The grasses growing halfway up the hedge had started to rebound from the crushing and it was mercifully impossible to trace the shape of a human body. He couldn't say whether the staining near the foot of the hedge was mud or blood, but when he had caressed a brown blade of grass he put his fingers on his tongue and thought he could taste that unique salty bitterness.

His eyes stinging with tears he turned away and went back through the gates. He was walking slowly towards the uniforms checking the few cars parked on the forecourt when his mobile rang. It was the leader of the car search team to report that Simon's hire car had been recovered. At first

144

sight it didn't offer anything significant, but it was of course awaiting the attention of Forensics. Absently Tim offered his congratulations, then stood watching the uniforms at work until he saw Ted and Bernard Charters coming through the door in the fence, Charters shrugging into an anorak. Tim thought he looked resigned but he was no fool, innocent or guilty he would have known a chat at the station was the inevitable next step.

After the offer of a cup of tea which he declined, Charters sat expressionless behind the table in the interview room, facing Tim and Ted.

In his usual slow, careful way, Ted activated the tape and intoned time, date and persons present.

"Now, Mr Charters . . ." Tim had to force himself to sound detached and relaxed. "I'd like to begin by showing you a photograph." It had been hard to ask his mother for the loan of it, and she had made him promise to return it before the day was out. The laser copy, he noted idly, was larger and sharper than the original, but with less depth. In his pocket, sharing an envelope with the original, was a second laser copy he had made for himself.

After a glance at him, his sergeant had taken the photograph from under his suddenly motionless fingers and turned it round to face Charters. "D'you recollect ever having seen this man, Mr Charters?" DS Mahy asked.

Charters had drawn back from the photograph in distaste, prepared, it was clear, for the picture of a corpse. As he looked reluctantly down at it his face cleared, and Tim was unable to see anything in it but relief as Charters studied Simon's bright, smiling face. The face which *he* should have been able to study, for years into the past and into the future.

Charters was shaking his head. He laid the photograph down on the table and swivelled it back to face the policemen.

"You're obviously asking me if I've seen him at the Golden Rose, and I suppose I may have done, but I don't remember, with the size of the crowd that's there every day at this time of year. I don't remember any individual, Inspector, Sergeant, unless something out of line happens over a sale, or I catch someone thieving."

"Or unless he or she has some distinguishing mark?"

"I might notice that at the time, but I'd be unlikely to remember it later." Charters paused, then continued speaking as if he had come to a decision. "I did notice my son yesterday afternoon talking to a young man who was sitting at a table just outside the indoor sales area. I remember vaguely that he was nice-looking and had very fair hair, but I was concentrating on my son, feeling pleased to see him chatting so freely, actually sitting down with the man at his table. He tends to be a solitary boy, self-sufficient, and I was glad . . ." The reminiscent pleasure disappeared from the man's face as it abruptly darkened. "But if it's the chap in this photograph he was on the job, wasn't he, trying to get at me through my boy? But I've nothing to hide, Inspector, as I'll tell you every time you ask me. I didn't set fire to my greenhouse. And I didn't kill the man the insurance company set on me. I had no reason to be afraid of him."

Tim leaned back in his chair, forcing himself to appear satisfied when all his instincts yearned to have Charters by the lapels. "Thank you, Mr Charters. That all sounds quite clear, and it's always a help when – people" – Tim's minimal pause was deliberate, and elicited a twitch of Charters' head as if he was shaking off a fly – "volunteer information. Now, when you were standing in the hall, wondering whether or not to give chase, you say you heard a vehicle engine? Heard it start up?"

"Yes!"

146

"You're sure?"

"Quite sure, Inspector."

"Would you have heard it if the car had been out in the lane?"

Charters appeared to be genuinely considering, and after a few seconds shook his head. "I doubt it, the forecourt's pretty wide."

"So the car must have been on the forecourt?"

"Yes . . ." For the second time the high forehead was ridged. "That's what I don't understand. Unless the man was thrown out of the car immediately it turned into the lane someone must have been following him."

A car somebody else was driving would be a very useful invention for Charters. But if he hadn't invented it he had to be right, the only other possibility was so remote: that one of the cars parked overnight on the Golden Rose forecourt had contained an awakened sleeper who had seen Simon running and either decided to follow him or simply decided it was time to go home. Someone who had perhaps been sleeping it off and had slewed into the hedge without intent . . . He himself had given his Chief a recent homily on the likelihood of coincidence.

But he couldn't believe in this one.

"So you just went back to bed, Mr Charters."

"Yes, Inspector." Charters' eyes were narrow and deep-set, but Tim could see that they were meeting his. "After checking the downstairs of my house for any loss or further damage, human nature being what it is. As I told you, I found neither." The eyes had slid down to the distressed table top, but Charters raised them again as he went on speaking. "You may have noticed some pieces of silver displayed in the sitting-room. And a rather good small combined radio, tape and CD player.

All highly portable. The usual type of burglar would surely have taken them."

"As I take your point, Mr Charters. Thank you." But the only thing Tim felt grateful for was that he didn't have to try and find out what type of burglar Simon had been. "I can tell you," he said after a moment's hesitation, "that the dead man was" – for an anguishing moment the past tense broke through his shield – "a private detective." He had just managed to give with one hand because of being about to take away with the other.

When he had indicated that the interview was terminated he told Charters he would want to talk to his wife and son as well, and enjoyed the sharp intake of breath and the flash of fear across the man's irritatingly camouflaged countenance. "I expect we shall want to talk to you again too, sir, when we have the reports on your clothes and the forensic examination of your house. For now, if you'll be good enough to go with my sergeant he'll arrange for you to be fingerprinted. It's just routine, sir, for purposes of elimination."

"Of course, Inspector."

Bernard Charters got to his feet without noticeable reaction, and Tim found himself disappointed that his chief suspect for the murder of his brother didn't appear to have needed the regulation reassurance.

Twelve

The pathologist's commentary on Simon's injuries made Tim skip lunch, but he forced himself to give Marjorie and Benjamin Charters time to have theirs before sending a car to bring them to the station for interview. WPC Joanne Torode was put in charge of the son while he and Ted were interviewing the mother, and he asked her to talk to the boy on subjects of his choice and be prepared to let him know her reactions to his reactions.

Marjorie Charters was more obviously on her guard than her husband had been, wary and self-protective. She neither added to nor altered anything her husband had told them, but Tim's sixth sense suggested she was afraid of more than she admitted to: a fear of the effect of an interview on her son.

"You'll be sitting beside him, Mrs Charters," Ted told her. Even when Tim didn't have to struggle minute by minute to retain his objectivity, he knew Ted's personality was the more reassuring. "And you say he was asleep while the intruder was in the house and didn't wake up until after he had left."

"That's right!" Tim was aware of Marjorie Charters' body tensing as she rapped out the words. Although it was a very different style of reaction, he was reminded of the over-elaborate nonchalance with which her husband had referred to the knee-hole desk in his study, and felt another stab of excitement as it reinforced his instinct that the Charter family had something to hide.

The boy was so tense he walked stiff-legged, and WPC Torode had shaken her head at Tim when he went in person to collect him, mute and white-faced, from the room where he and the WPC had been alone together during his mother's interview.

"I don't suppose you can tell me anything about last night that your parents haven't already told me," were his first words to the boy when he was sitting rigid beside his mother. Not believing Ted capable of easing up on his invariably portentous opening to a tape, Tim had announced it himself in as light a manner as possible. "Seeing that you slept through the disturbance of the intruder. That's right, isn't it, Benjamin?"

"Yes."

"The cat ran howling up the stairs, the table in the hall fell over and a vase shattered on the parquet, but none of these things wakened you. So you're a heavy sleeper?"

"He is, Mr Le Page!"

He had known the mother would answer. Most parents did, until invited not to. "If you'll just let Benjamin speak for himself, Mrs Charters," he suggested, as gently as he could manage. "It's a requirement of his interview." Tim turned back to the boy. "You're a heavy sleeper, then, Benjamin?"

"I think so. But I keep my door closed and go a long way down in the bedclothes."

"I see. Did you wake up when your father came back upstairs?"

The boy's face shot round to look at his mother, and Tim was aware of a flash of panic. But when she told him to take his time, that the inspector had to ask him that sort of question, he turned back to the policemen and told them calmly and while

looking into Tim's eyes that he hadn't wakened up until his
mother had come to call him as usual at half past seven.

"Thank you, Benjamin. Did your mother tell you then about
what had happened in the night?"

"Sort of." This time the boy spoke unprompted, without
looking to his mother. "She said . . . someone had come
into the house through the kitchen window but my Dad had
heard and frightened him away before he had time to steal
anything."

"I see." Tim glanced at Marjorie Charters as the boy
stopped speaking, and wondered if he could see relief in
her face as well as approval of her son's performance. But
he knew from past experience how easy it was to think he
saw things he wished to see. "Thank you, Benjamin. And
when did you first learn that the intruder had been killed in
the lane?" *The intruder.* His brother. The brother he hadn't
known he had until he didn't have him . . . Savagely Tim
pulled himself back to the interview.

"When two policemen came to tell us. They asked if we'd
heard anything unusual in the night, and then Dad told them,
and about the broken things in the hall."

"Were you surprised that your Dad hadn't been intending
to tell the police about the break-in?" The boy stared at him in
silence, eyes wide in what looked like terror. "Benjamin?"

Tim saw the mother's throat move, but to his grudging
admiration she remained silent. After a glance at her, Benjamin
turned back to the policemen and whispered, "No."

"Why not?" DS Mahy prompted.

"Because he knew it was the insurance people. They'll stoop
to anything to save themselves having to pay out." It had to
be a quote from his parents. "So what would have been the
point?" That, too. And maybe because they had asked him to

151

learn certain things by heart. "But when we heard somebody was dead . . ." The sound that followed could have been a sob or a hiccup.

"When did you learn that somebody was dead, Benjamin?"

"I've told you. When the police came and told us."

The boy had answered pat, and if he had answered truthfully there would have been no need for the terror to come back into his eyes before he slid his gaze down to the table top. Tim felt another stab of excitement. "Yes, of course." For the time being he was satisfied. Marjorie Charters drew a shuddering breath as he pronounced that the interview was terminated, and studied his face with surprise and suspicion in her own.

"Don't you or your husband flee the island," DS Mahy advised her, "we'll maybe want to talk to you again." If Tim had a fault to find with his admirable DS, it was an occasional insensitivity that emerged as a jokiness which had the opposite effect on the interviewee from the one Ted had to be intending. Marjorie Charters bridled as she got to her feet and pulled her son up with her.

"I don't think that's something you need worry about."

"Of course not," Tim said heartily. "My sergeant likes his little joke." Ted smiled, unchastened. He would do it again. "Thank you both for coming in."

When he got back to his office he rang the hospital and was told that his mother was no longer there: his wife, unable to get hold of him, had left a message to tell him she had taken her home. Looking at his watch he was astonished to see that it was evening, and left immediately for Rouge Rue.

The quiet pastel morning had expanded into a hot summer's day, but his mother looked pale and cold in his north-facing sitting-room, lying on the huge old sofa in a loose-fitting white wrap. Duffy was stretched out on the floor beside her, and Tim saw that he rose slowly and stiffly before coming over to the door to welcome him – his first intimation that his dog was growing old.

And when his mother looked up at him, the intimation sharpened into a bleak awareness of all mortality as he saw how gaunt her face had grown. But each hour since he had last seen her felt like a day and a night, and he could imagine there had been time for his brother's death to take a visible toll.

"Oh, Tim, please don't mind, I couldn't stand another moment in that hospital." Her voice had lost its purr. "Anna's in the kitchen making a sandwich. We neither of us wanted anything at lunchtime, here or at the hospital, but she decided it was time we made an effort."

"I'm very glad to have you home." He bent to kiss her cheek, not knowing whether or not he meant it. "I didn't want anything at lunchtime, either, but I'll make an effort with you. Tell me first, though . . ." He pushed his grandmother's beaded stool towards her with his foot, and squatted down on it. "Did Simon tell you he was going to pay the Golden Rose a second open visit? I'm sorry, Mother, but I'll need to ask—"

"It's all right, Tim. I know you're a policeman and I want you to find out who killed him." Her determinedly reassuring smile made him as uneasy as her stony gaze into space before she had been aware of his presence. "Yes, he did. But he didn't tell me what he was going to do last night, although he hinted he might go undercover before he left. How do you know he was at the place during the day?"

"He rang his London insurance contact from there on his mobile. Told him he would go in during the night if he could get in without breaking in. If he didn't tell

153

you he won't have told anyone else. I'd better go and see Anna."

Anna was the weak point in his new armour, and he went out to the kitchen with a dreadful, unfamiliar sensation of reluctance. She was making sandwiches with cucumber and what looked like corned beef. "Sandwiches are easiest when you're not hungry," she said conversationally, glancing up briefly from the work surface. "Are you getting anywhere?"

"Nowhere I can put into words. But my instincts tell me the Charters are hiding something. I felt the boy had been rehearsed, though he didn't appear to have seen or heard anything. And the mother was desperately defensive."

"What next, then? Have you contacted the insurance company Simon was working for?" Anna put down the knife as she spoke and turned to put her hands on his shoulders. Warily he put his round her waist.

"Yes. His contact's coming over to see the Chief and me tomorrow. It appears Simon rang him yesterday afternoon from the Golden Rose to tell him he'd decided to go in if he could manage it without breaking anything. He didn't tell even Mother, so perhaps it was a spur of the moment decision."

"Because something had happened? Oh, darling, I'm sorry, you don't know . . ."

"No. And I never will."

Tim couldn't remember the last time he had cried. If crying was the word for the dry rasping sobs that were suddenly shivering through him. But although his wife had been their catalyst, holding her in his arms was helping him through them. It was several moments before they ceased.

"I'm sorry." He drew back on a last shuddering breath as Anna tried to keep her relief out of her face. "At least this

154

Mr Taylor may be able to tell us something about Simon's mission and what his thinking on it was."

"Yes. D'you want a sandwich?"

He wanted to thank her for being so matter-of-fact about his brief unmanning, but that would be to negate her sense of fitness. "I'll try."

The three of them tried, with lots of coffee, and were still toying when Tim gave a yell and knocked his plate to the floor as he flung his arms ceilingwards. Crusts scattered across the old multi-coloured rug as he dropped to his knees and edged over to the sofa.

"It's all right, it's all right!" He turned to reassure Anna as well, but too late to save her from another wave of cold that made her physically shudder. "It's just that I suddenly thought . . ." He seized his mother's hand. "I've not been behaving like a policeman *or* a brother. For God's sake, Mother, I don't even know if Simon had a partner. If he was *married*!"

"He *was* married." The reminiscent sorrow in her eyes made him look away from her. "Very early, very briefly, and very misguidedly. No children, and he hasn't seen her for years. Since then there have just been girlfriends, no living in. When I – used to ask him" – she had pulled his hand against her, and he was aware of a quick succession of short breaths – "he said he hadn't found anyone who could cope with his lifestyle. So there's no one else to contact, darling. If there had been, I'd have done it, or told Gina to."

"Of course." Tim slowly withdrew his hand and edged back to his chair. "Normally the incident room team collect what autobiographical material they can on a murder victim, but Simon was left to me as a friend of the family. All I had to do was question his mother, but I didn't do it."

"You've done it just a few hours after the investigation began," Anna ventured. She had felt wary in conversation with her husband for a mere matter of hours, but the sensation was already disagreeably familiar. "An incident room team could hardly have been quicker. And you knew Lorna would tell you anything that could be significant."

"There isn't anything outside his assignment from the insurance company," Lorna said, following Tim's impatient nod towards his wife, "that I know of. Simon didn't confide his every move to Gina or to me, but he was more susceptible than you've ever been, Tim. There always seemed to be girlfriends. But no special one since his divorce. And no other extra-curricular activity known to us that could have had anything to do with – with what's happened. I asked Gina when I spoke to her from the hospital."

"Of course you did. Thanks, Mother. Now, I'm afraid I'll have to go out again. I'm not sure when I'll be back but it shouldn't be late." He pictured himself, before he returned to them, driving to a remote piece of coast and running himself physically exhausted. He would probably do it.

While they were clearing the crumbs Anna told him she needed a few things from the supermarket and Lorna said she'd be fine on her own. When Anna had left Tim remained standing in front of the sofa, shuffling his feet.

"What are you finding difficult to say, darling?"

"That I don't want you to open the door to anyone, unless you can see through the window that it's Clare, say, or Robin, or anyone else you know apart from Constance Lorimer. I can't think she would come after you again, but if she isn't quite sane and finds out you've left the Princess Elizabeth . . ." And if he got to her house and she wasn't there . . . "Anyway, it looks now as if it could have been Simon whoever it was was after outside the Duke."

"I think it was Constance. After me. I'll go on thinking that, Tim, unless you can prove it wasn't."

"So the way Simon – was killed . . . That was a coincidence?"

"It has to be."

"I'll find out. I will, darling. And meanwhile you promise not to open the door unless you're sure who it is?"

"I promise."

"The side gate's locked, so no one can get to the back door, you'll be okay in the garden if you feel like a change, and it's a glorious evening." His thoughts were already racing towards his next concern, but he forced himself to hold them back. "There aren't any real hazards between here and the garden, you should be able to walk—"

"Tim!" For the first time since the news of Simon's death, it was a real smile. "It's my shoulder I dislocated, not my leg, and I've stayed in this house before. Now, off you *go!*"

Although it was almost six o'clock the heat hit him on the doorstep, rebounding from brick and stone and stucco. The thought of Constance Lorimer's house, of its owner perhaps eating a meal, made him feel sick in anticipation, but he was so eager to get there he felt a rare frustration with the small, slow road system whose quickly changing borders he usually so much enjoyed. As he passed Beth Smith's immaculate home he saw that the outer door was shut, and found himself surprised when Constance's battered front door was jarred open without a diffused blonde aureole appearing behind the stained-glass sunburst.

"What do *you* want?"

It was Constance glaring at him from the threshold, looking

as though she had commanded it motionless for years, the only movement the smoke drifting upwards from the cigarette stuck to her pouting lower lip.

"Another word with you, Mrs Lorimer. This time about a murder." Unless she or Beth had listened to the lunchtime news he would be giving her a shock. If she hadn't committed the murder herself, of course. Either way, Tim thought wearily, she was unlikely to vouchsafe him a reaction, genuine or feigned.

He saw her eyelids flicker, and even against the gloom behind her he was sure her squat body had jerked, but she spoke with her usual loud harsh scorn. "So? What do you think a murder has to do with me?"

"I don't know, Mrs Lorimer, that's why I want to talk to you. May I come in?"

It was the last thing he wanted, but he had to be glad when she leaned past him, her mustiness enveloping him like the furry dust turning in the sun shaft that disappeared as she closed the door behind him. Slowly, then, she turned and led the way towards her sitting-room, her legs toiling like uprooted stems. Their passage across the malodorous hall seemed unending, but again there was the slight relief of an open window. Replanted with her back to the fireplace and having lit a fresh cigarette from the old one, Constance waved him to a chair.

"So, then, Mr Le Page," she said as he sat gingerly down. "Someone has despatched that mother of yours at last."

He wanted to get up again, put his hands round her brown, thickly-veined neck, and squeeze. If he could bring himself to touch her. "My mother wasn't the victim this time, Mrs Lorimer. A young friend of our family who came over for my wedding, Simon Shaw, was run down and killed in the

158

Vale in the middle of last night, close to the Golden Rose garden centre."

He hadn't expected a visible reaction, certainly not the cackle of laughter. It ended in a bout of rheumy coughing as Mrs Lorimer choked on cigarette smoke. "And you think I knew where her boyfriend would be, and at what precise time," she croaked at last, before hawking so explicitly Tim had to swallow a sudden excess of saliva. "Tell me how I discovered that, Mr Le Page."

"I can't, Mrs Lorimer." Because he hadn't the faintest idea.

She was nodding in agreement. "Of course you can't. But I suppose you want to take my car again?"

"Yes." Tim realised as he spoke that he had wanted to take Constance Lorimer's car into custody since the moment he had heard the news of Simon's death, but it was only when he had got into his own car in Rouge Rue that he had given in to the weakest of his current instincts and used his mobile to ask for it to be impounded again. Probably uselessly, by now: if she had run Simon down, he had allowed her time to wash it. But the guilty car this time had been in collision with a hedge as well as a human body, and there was just the chance it might have collected a tell-tale mark she would be unable to remove.

If the murder victim hadn't been his brother, would he be in her house now? Knowing her history *vis-à-vis* his mother, he thought that he would and felt suddenly on surer ground, wishing he had brought Ted with him so that the interview could have been official. As it was, he would have to log his visit as no more than a courtesy call to inform Mrs Lorimer that her car was to be impounded

159

for the second time. "And, you see, it was Mr Shaw who pulled my mother back from the other hit-and-run incident in L'Hyvreuse. We have to consider the possibility of a connection."

"If there's a connection, Mr Le Page, it's the proof of my innocence. Until you arrived just now I didn't so much as know the name of your mother's latest." Her eyes, which had held his from the moment she had asked him to sit down, seemed to intensify their gaze. It was impossible to know if she was speaking the truth.

"This is an informal chat, Mrs Lorimer, and everything you've said to me is off the record. We'll leave it there for the moment." He had to look away from her to be able to get to his feet. "Miss Smith not with you today," he commented, as with an uncommunicative grunt she began her return plough across the once-white carpet.

She answered him as she put her hand out to the front door. "Miss Smith doesn't live in my pocket. She'll be with her young man. Lorna Le Page isn't the only one."

"Young man?"

Constance Lorimer's sniff was as rheumy as her cough. It felt like fantasy to think that she had been married to Simon's father. "Her handyman she calls him, and perhaps that's the right word for him, it covers everything he does for her." This time it was her scorn that intensified her gaze. "You didn't know that, did you? You looked on the surface and you saw an old maid. But that's not Beth, she gives herself a good life." Bizarrely, Tim was aware of Constance Lorimer's vicarious pride in her friend's achievement, the only emotion beyond her scorn of him and his mother he was sure he had correctly interpreted.

160

"And spends plenty of it with you, Mrs Lorimer."

Against the light from outside he saw her complacent shrug. "I can't complain, she's a good friend. When can I expect to lose my car again, Mr Le Page?"

"At any moment."

"It hasn't been out of the garage since they brought it back last time. You'll be wasting your time."

"Murder investigations always involve a waste of time."

Now she was smiling, a rictus of the lips which had her cigarette wobbling. If she had killed Simon, the essential second car wash could be disguised as the first. Simon's clothes had been geared to leave no traces, and all he could hope for, apart from vestiges of the Vale flora, was that someone from the forensic team might have a sufficiently good memory to spot a new wound among the old scars on the body of the car, and have a good enough photo of the front nearside to back it up . . .

He wasn't surprised to see Constance Lorimer still smiling as he looked back at her from the gate. Beth Smith's car was in her driveway when he reached her house, and she was turning left on foot out of her gate, towards Constance's. He had hardly gathered speed and was able to look her in the face for a moment as she paused, stared, and then smiled in recognition. It was obvious to her where he had been, and he saw the minimal shrug of her thin shoulders as she went on her way. He thought he had also seen more colour in her face and a fullness to her lips which he hadn't noticed before, but that could be simply because what Constance had said about her had made him look at her in a different way.

It was still Constance who remained smiling in his mind's eye to irritate him as he gathered speed, but when he stopped in a layby and answered his mobile the lingering image of her disappeared.

Ted told him there was recently deposited blood matching Simon's on both sleeves of the anorak they had impounded from Bernard Charters.

Thirteen

At half-past eight the report came through: none of the three members of the Charters family were of the same blood group as Simon.

It made things a great deal easier. Tim reluctantly sent the wife and the son home and then, with DS Mahy, called Bernard Charters into an interview room, put in a tape, and told him the news.

Charters made no verbal response, but Tim, closely observing the non-hirsute parts of his face, saw his Adam's apple jerk sharply up and down and a tic start work under an eye.

"So there's only one explanation possible, Mr Charters: you were in physical contact with the dead man after he had received his injuries. I really don't think there is any point in denying it. Take your time."

For a few seconds there was no reaction, then Charters' chest rose and fell in a deep sigh and he leaned forward, resting his elbows on the table top and his chin on his clasped hands.

"I did go out to the lane," he said, quietly but clearly. "And I did go up to the body. I – I was so shocked I don't know exactly what I did then, but if you found blood on my sleeves . . . I must have touched it. Perhaps I put my hands on the shoulders for a moment . . . I'm not sure."

"We think you did something much more specific with your

hands than that, Mr Charters. There was a camera on a cord round the murdered man's neck. It appears from marks on the back of the neck that someone tried to break the cord. When they were unable to, they opened the camera and took the film out. The camera was still open when we found the body, and there was no film in it." When he said 'body' or 'murdered man' he could just manage to turn his near-constant mental image of Simon's lifeless face into a blank. "I think you removed that film, Mr Charters."

"You found my fingerprints?"

"We found evidence on the camera that someone had used cloth to obliterate any. They succeeded, but I don't really think that helps you."

"What *do* you really think, Inspector Le Page?" Bernard Charters had thrown himself back in the chair he was too big for, and Tim was aware that he had suddenly relaxed, perhaps into the calmness of despair. "That I followed the man by car when he ran from my house, drove into him, backed down the lane, drove on to my forecourt where I left the car, then came out again on foot to see what damage I'd done?"

"That could be it in a nutshell." Ted nodded his approval.

"But it isn't what happened." In another extravagant movement Charters was leaning across the table. "I did come out, but only on foot. And I only touched – the body – because the face was unmarked and the injuries were hidden in the clothes and I thought he might still be alive."

"And when you found he was dead you went back home to bed. You weren't going to tell the police about the man entering your house, and you weren't going to tell them you'd found his body."

"The police found the body soon enough. And as I already

164

told you – I wasn't leaving a burglar free to break into other houses. He was only interested in me."

"So you tell us." Tim suddenly realised how tired he was, although he couldn't envisage sleeping, being able to shut out the heartrending, irremediable thing that had happened.

"Were you aware that you had bloodstains on your jacket, Mr Charters?" Ted was asking.

"I didn't think whether I had or not, it was so ghastly. Like a nightmare." Charters shot upright. "If I'd killed the man, Mr Le Page, I'd have thought then, wouldn't I? I'd have washed the jacket, or I'd have destroyed or dumped it. Isn't that something in my favour?"

It had to be. Tim was glad that Ted stepped in. "It's amazing what one can overlook at a time of stress, Mr Charters. But yes, we're aware you made no attempt to wash or destroy the jacket you wore."

"You're sure there's nothing else that you'd like to tell us?" Tim inquired.

"Nothing else." But Charter's deep-set gaze shifted down to the table top as he spoke, and Tim's instinct that he was still holding something back was restored.

"I shall want an amended statement, Mr Charters. Then you're free to go." He would have liked to interview the wife and son again as well, but felt it would be heavy-handed at that juncture. And there might be something to learn in the morning from the London insurance agent.

"Care for a beer, sir?" Ted asked, as he joined Tim in the office after handing Bernard Charters over to a uniform. "Cordammy, I'm not thinking, you'll be wanting to get back to your bride. A rotten way to spend a honeymoon, Tim, I'm really sorry. You know, the Chief wouldn't have insisted—"

"I was the one who insisted, Ted. Simon Shaw was a good

friend." He hated belittling Simon's significance. But perhaps eventually he might feel he could tell Ted what that was. When the case was closed and no one was in a position to take him off it. That was why he didn't want to sit with Ted over beers at the moment, not because he wanted to go home.

But he told Ted that was where he was going, thanked him for being so thoughtful, and set off across the island to the west coast.

The temperature had dropped during the day, and a wind had come up. The change suited his uneasy mood. He parked by Grandes Rocques and walked south towards Cobo, running when he was on springy turf and taking his shoes and socks off when he came to the shore. He even paddled at the edge of the receding tide, then sat on a pink rock as dusk turned to dark and the last of the day's holiday-makers trickled away. He had seated himself so that he could measure the coming of the night against the dark green bulk of Le Guet, the wooded headland forming the southern end of Cobo Bay, and watched it until its dark green daylight detail had faded to featureless black. When he eventually got to his feet there was one star just above the faint grey horizon, which by the time he had put on his shoes and socks and walked briskly back to his car was obscured by the blown strands of cloud puffing up the sky.

When he got into the car he was shivering, and feeling lonely in a way that only a year ago would have been impossible. As he knew with a rush of relief that it meant he was wanting his wife, he realised the perverseness of his resentment against her that she hadn't lost a brother. For God's sake, she had lost an only son.

He could hardly wait to get home. Anna was in her chair by the sitting-room grate, and there was a low flame on the gas fire defying the sudden chill of the evening. She was gazing at it, and when she heard him in the doorway and looked up he was shocked and ashamed to see an uncertainty in her eyes he had never seen there before. He rushed across the room and cast himself down at her feet, pushing his body gently between her knees in the familiar movement which since their marriage he had not made. To his infinite gratitude they were as compliant as always, and he laid his head on them.

"I'm sorry, darling. I've been a pig."

"No. You've been bereaved and bewildered. I understand."

"I know you do. You and Mother both. How is she?"

"All right. I sat with her a while when she was in bed and she seemed ready to sleep. She's happier here than in the hospital. Can you tell me what happened this evening?"

He told her about the change in Bernard Charters' statement. "I believe he took that film. Which has to mean he had something in his house he didn't want photographed. No doubt by now it's in an impregnable place and the film destroyed, but I'll ask for a search warrant tomorrow. When I've seen the man from London."

"Have you eaten?"

He considered in surprise. "Not since that sandwich. I didn't think. And anyway, there wasn't time." He had no need to tell her, now, that there had been time to walk by the sea.

"Bacon and egg, then?"

Tim hesitated before saying yes, because absurdly it seemed disloyal to Simon. But there would be a better chance of sleep if he had something in his belly. Anna sat with him while he ate at the kitchen table, and afterwards they went up to bed and lay affectionately in one another's arms, each with a sense of relief to ease the sense of sorrow.

In the early morning, the night to Tim seemed to have been a long series of painful rememberings tempered by Anna's embrace, but he was no longer tired and the energy of his resolve to discover the truth of Simon's death felt stronger than ever. When he opened his eyes he saw that Anna was looking at him in the soft grey light filtering through the thin curtains, and as he smiled at her he was relieved to see the restored confidence in her face.

"I'm going to work this morning, Tim, if Lorna feels like she did at bedtime. I'm sure she'll be all right for a few hours."

"She never lived in this house, so it doesn't have uncomfortable memories. Duffy and Whitby will help. Could you give Duffy a run later?"

"Of course. If it suits Lorna I'll take them both somewhere in the car where there's a seat and she can get out and sit while Duffy and I stretch our legs." Anna sat up. "D'you feel like taking the dog out now?"

"Yes! Why don't we both— Oh no, Mother . . ."

"Go on your own. Tea and toast first?"

He kissed her. "When I get back."

It was barely six o'clock when he went out to the garage, but the sun was dazzling off the windows opposite and already held some warmth. As he drove north he had to force himself not to think of the fun it would have been to show Simon his beloved island. On L'Ancresse Common he let his obedient dog run free and for a few moments emulated his pace on the dry grass, aware as always of the nearness of the sea. The only other living creatures within sight apart from the birds were a couple of tame tethered nanny-goats used to human company, who nuzzled his hand in friendly fashion while keeping a wary eye on a respectfully distant Duffy. When he got home at seven he was ready for his usual small breakfast, and as ready as he felt he could be for whatever the working day might bring.

He was at the office by nine, and it seemed a long wait for Ian Taylor, Simon's contact at the head office of the insurance company who had engaged him. There was nothing more to be done with the murder case pending his arrival, and Tim found it difficult to concentrate on other matters. But with the restoration of high summer flying conditions were perfect, and a taxi delivered the man from London as scheduled, in time for a slightly delayed mid-morning coffee.

In the Chief's office, as Tim poured from a cafetière into the station's best bone china, Ian Taylor expressed his sorrow at the fate of the man he had employed. "He was recommended to us and I liked and trusted him immediately, despite his youth. It's a tragedy. And of course I can't help feeling responsible."

Tim was reluctantly silent, and after a glance at him the Chief responded. "If you urged Shaw to break the law and enter the Charters' house you *are* partly responsible, Mr Taylor." Tim saw the man from London flinch. "If you left him to carry out the job for which you had engaged him as he thought fit, the responsibility was his."

Ian Taylor was silent for what to Tim felt like a very long time. Then he bowed his head and spoke softly to his lap. "I'd intended telling you that I'd left him free to decide what methods he would use, but he's dead because of what I asked him to do, and I find I have to tell you the truth. Simon Shaw entered the Charters' premises because I persuaded him. But he refused to go in if he found that it would involve any breakage or lock-picking. Evidently it didn't."

There was another silence and then the Chief, without comment, handed Taylor a couple of A4 sheets. "This is an account of events that night so far as we are sure of them. But I've no doubt you'd like us to go over them with you now."

"If you will, Chief Inspector." Ian Taylor was a big man

169

with a lot of grey hair and a thin face with a generous mouth. A man who in normal circumstances would have disposed Tim to like him, but who now was the most hated being whose company he had ever been forced to endure.

When the Chief and Tim, between them, had told him what they could, leaving out by prior agreement the fact of Tim's friendship with the deceased, the Chief asked him if there was any specific reason why his company had felt the need to investigate the Charters' claim so drastically.

"There were two main reasons." Taylor leaned forward in the Chief's best armchair. "The size of the sum involved, and the fact that the pictures had been moved to the greenhouse from their approved place in the house without our being informed. So our investigations have been on two fronts: the true value of the pictures, and what caused the fire. The damage to the greenhouse was so severe it's impossible to determine the source of the fire, but we felt we had some scope as regards the pictures, which we underwrote on the strength of the authentication certificates which Mr Charters tells us were destroyed with them. So we contacted all Guernsey picture dealers in case any of them had known the pictures and had professional views on them, and discovered that the Charters had made an appointment to have them revalued by a firm in St Peter Port. All details there." Ian Taylor in his turn laid some papers on the Chief's desk.

"When pressed, the firm told us the owners had been disturbed by the unsolicited judgment of a friend of theirs, the local amateur art critic Henry Thomas. Mr Thomas was reluctant to tell tales, as he expressed it, but, again when pressed, he told us reluctantly that he remained convinced the pictures were nineteenth-century fakes." Taylor paused to drink coffee.

"Mr Thomas also told us," he resumed, "that he saw

nothing adversely significant about the removal of the pictures to the greenhouse: the cupboard there offered the right
conditions for storage, and Charters had been concerned for
the safety of the pictures following a couple of recent art
burglaries. We gathered from Thomas that no member of
the Charters family liked the pictures, and their removal
from the house satisfied them on aesthetic grounds as well."
Taylor had looked stricken since the Chief's uncompromis-
ing indictment, but the twitch now at the corner of his mouth
confirmed Tim's grudging impression that he had a sense of
humour. "The St Peter Port art expert agreed with Thomas
that the pictures were properly stored. I gathered during my
conversations with both men that Guernsey greenhouses are
used for a great many purposes since the tomato industry
slackened off."

"That's true," Tim forced himself to reply automatically
before carrying on with a surge of adrenalin-producing hope.
"Mr Taylor, the insurance angle of the fire wasn't a police
matter, so we were unaware of events immediately following
it. Did you come to the island yourself and see these art
experts? See the Charters?" His Chief had turned sharply
towards him, and Tim knew he must work harder to keep
his excitement out of his voice.

"Yes. For the reasons I've just given you."

"And. . . Did you. . . did you have any feeling that the Charters could be hiding something? Were not just straightforwardly
distressed by their loss?"

"This is a murder inquiry now, Mr Taylor, and it will be
helpful if we can collect feelings as well as facts." Tim couldn't
have put it better himself, and it was a relief that his Chief was
backing him up, not seeing his request as the out-of-line plea
of partiality.

171

"Yes, of course." Ian Taylor leaned back in his chair, contemplating. "I don't know," he said slowly, after a moment's silence. "I was aware of a great deal of tension in all three members of the family, but that could have been fear of the future without their financial safety net, I suppose. They certainly told a clear and consistent story, and stuck to it."

"Their garden centre is very popular," Tim said. "And I've heard they were anxious to expand. That could have been their main reason for deciding to sell the pictures."

"And the incentive, perhaps, for fraud if they were suddenly afraid the pictures weren't going to bring the money they needed." Tim was glad it was his Chief who had said it.

"Precisely." Ian Taylor leaned forward, for the first time looking hesitant and exclusively addressing the Chief. "I don't suppose . . . Are you in a position at the moment to tell me anything about the progress of the murder inquiry?"

"I'm afraid not." The Chief answered without hesitation. "You know from his last telephone call to you that Mr Shaw had agreed to enter the Charters' house if he found an opening and we are confident that he did, before meeting his death from a car in the lane outside the Golden Rose. We can also tell you that he had a camera on a cord round his neck, and that when he was found the camera was open and had no film in it. Beyond that . . . I'm afraid you'll have to keep your inquiry on hold, Mr Taylor, if you feel it to be dependent on discovering how your agent died."

It was as near as they could go to predicating Bernard Charters' guilt, and Ian Taylor knew it. He leaned back with a sigh. "Thank you, Chief Inspector, I understand. And that you wouldn't advise me to call on the Charters family during this particular visit."

Death of a Stranger

"I think not," the Chief said mildly. Tim saw the gleam of relief in his eyes that the man was making it so easy.

"Very well." Taylor got to his feet and the policemen followed suit. "Chief Inspector . . ." Taylor held out his hands, uncertainty sitting uneasily on his seasoned face. "Is there . . . Have I committed an offence?"

"Unfortunately we have no means of discovering that, Mr Taylor. But I hope you will see your directions to Mr Shaw as constituting one. Inspector, will you take Mr Taylor to Reception and get them to order him a taxi?" Taylor half held out his hand, but the Chief didn't take it.

When he had handed him over, Tim went back to the Chief's office.

The Chief was looking out towards the tree, and as he turned round he and Tim regarded one another in silence.

"How are you, Tim?" the Chief asked eventually. His face was kind.

"I'm all right, sir."

"Good. Now, you'd better get on."

"Yes, sir."

It was just possible he might be able to tell the Chief as well, when it was all over.

173

Fourteen

B enjamin Charters had gone to bed with his mind in a
turmoil, but when he was wakened by his mother at
his usual time, after a dreamless sleep he had not expected,
he knew what he had to do. Although the prospect was
terrifying, the sense of a decision reached after so much
unhappy heart-searching made him feel calmer than he had
felt since the nightmare began.

"You look better, Benjamin," his father said at the breakfast table.

His father looked terrible. Even worse than he had looked
the night before. Benjamin had been allowed to wait up with
his mother for his return from the police station, and as he
came up to the kitchen door where they were waiting, alerted
by the sound of the car, Benjamin had thought he looked like
an old man, his shoulders bent and his face grey.

"The blood," his father had said while his mother was gently
taking off his coat. "It's the same group as the dead man, and
different from all of ours."

His mother had moaned, and Benjamin hadn't been able
to tell which of them was helping the other into the sitting-
room.

"So what could you say?" his mother asked, when she and
his father were side by side and hand in hand on the sofa,
and he was squatted on the pouffe in front of them.

174

"I had to tell them I'd gone out – on foot – and gone up to the body. They accused me of removing the film and I denied it." Now a sound had escaped Benjamin, and his father looked at him sharply. "What is it, son?"

"Did they believe you?" the boy whispered.

"They didn't say." His father gave a harsh bark of laughter, free of all amusement. "They did say someone had success-fully obliterated any fingerprints from the camera."

This time it was his mother who laughed, so shrilly Benjamin exclaimed again.

Now they ignored him, turning to each other. "That's all right, then," his mother said.

"I didn't think you were a fool, Marjorie." His father spoke so scornfully the boy as well as his mother shrank away from him. "Of course it's not all right. Who else could they put in the frame?"

She had shaken her head without speaking, and Benjamin had been unable to sit looking at their misery any longer and had taken himself off to bed. Besides, he needed to think, to decide whether he should do the one thing that he could do. Tell the truth. He didn't know how much it would help, but his parents had brought him up to believe that the truth helped everyone. And he had seen it working in their lives. Until now.

And it was his fault that it wasn't working still.

Perhaps it was the weight of that which had brought him to the morning's decision. Or perhaps it was just that he couldn't live with his responsibility any more. Whatever it was, his mind was made up and now he must do it as quickly as possible.

"I'm going for a ride," he mumbled, as his mother got to her feet and began to clear the breakfast table. "I'd like to stretch my legs." That was how his parents put it when they

175

decided they wanted the exercise he himself never felt any need of.

Both of them said "Good!" and looked at him with surprise. In the days before the nightmare had started they had always been coaxing him to use his bike more, get out and about instead of sitting in that greenhouse . . .

His father was murmuring. "If they come with a search warrant . . ."

He had to get there first. "See you later," he said, jumping up. "I'll just get a hanky," he lied as he left the kitchen at a run.

Up in his parents' bedroom, treading softly in case they went into the sitting-room beneath, he cautiously lifted the extension telephone. Thank goodness he didn't have to look up the number, the taxi firm sent a car for him nearly every day during term-time, because of his parents being busy at the centre. He asked for one in five minutes, told them where it should wait. They said they'd do their best. Then he went into his own room and took enough money to pay the taxi out of his tight-lidded tin, glad now that the nightmare had taken away his appetite for ice-creams. He called goodbye as he ran through the kitchen. His mother had sat down at the table again after clearing it and they were both slumped hopelessly in their chairs.

It was a warm dry morning, he had no need of a jacket. He took his bike from the toolshed, realising when he saw the film of dust how long it was since he'd used it. Normally he would have at least flipped the seat with his handkerchief because he was a clean and tidy boy, but today he climbed straight on to the saddle, rode round the deserted building, across the forecourt and out into the lane.

The summer tourist season was the time of risk to property,

but he'd stowed his bike at all times of the year in the ditch up the crack off the lane just before it joined what on the island passed for a main road, and it had always been there when he came back for it after taking the bus into St Sampson for an ice-cream and a stroll round the shops. He'd lied then, Benjamin reflected unhappily, as he plodded the remaining few yards of the lane, telling his parents when he got home what a long, healthy ride he'd had, and for the first time he began to suspect that telling the truth at all times was a hard thing for everyone, however old or young you were.

The taxi arrived a couple of minutes after he reached the corner. He had hoped he wouldn't know the driver but he did; it was the young one who in normal times he liked best.

"Running away from home are we, then?" the driver asked. Benjamin jumped guiltily before realising it was a joke, not a real question.

"Just thought I'd get a bit of exercise and save you the turn," he heard himself say. Another lie. When he said he wanted to go to the police station the man raised an eyebrow and looked slightly curious, but he merely said, "Okay," and shrugged as Benjamin got into the back. Normally he sat in the front, but today he didn't want to talk to anyone until he'd talked to Detective Inspector Le Page. The driver didn't say anything on the journey either and Benjamin admired his restraint: the discovery of the murder had been too late for the *Press*, but he and his mother had watched the Channel TV report in anguish the night before.

When they arrived on the station forecourt the driver did say, "You're sure you're all right, now?" as Benjamin leaned in through the open window to pay him, and Benjamin thought there was anxiety as well as amusement in his eyes. For an

177

unrealistic happy moment, he imagined explaining things to him when everything was all right again.

"I'm fine. Honestly. Thanks."

"Want a ride back?"

He hadn't thought about it, but now he did, he was certain the detective inspector would see to that.

If he allowed him to go home.

"No, thanks."

"Okay, Master Charters. See you."

It could be that the driver would contact his parents to ease his conscience that he might have been aiding and abetting some ill-advised escapade. But Benjamin didn't care. By the time anyone caught up with him, he would have done what he had come to do.

It was a boost that the policeman on Reception recognised him, was round the counter shepherding him along the corridor almost before he had got out his request to see the detective inspector. They encountered DI Le Page in his office doorway.

"Young man to see you, sir," the PC said, and Benjamin saw the DI's face sharpen, suddenly intent.

"Benjamin!" he said, as suddenly smiling. But he didn't have to be careful, Benjamin had made up his mind. "You're with your father?"

"I'm on my own. I came in a taxi. My mother and father don't know I'm here." He heard himself speaking in a fluent rush, not stumbling over his words as he usually did when it mattered. "There's something I've got to tell you."

"Of course. We'll find an interview room. Get hold of DS Mahy, will you?" he ordered the PC. Benjamin could see that the detective inspector had been reluctant to take his eyes off him and fix them even for a second on the police constable

178

who was escorting him, and realised that part of his tension now was excitement, pleasure even, at finding himself the focus of the attention of someone important.

But there was still the fact that he was only twelve years old. Benjamin heard the DI ask for a social worker to be brought in with a sense of deflation. But the DI then said, "Soonest!" very sharply and his sense of worth was restored. Not that that was why he had come, he hadn't thought of himself, for once, in making his decision to tell the truth. To do the one thing that must finally persuade the insurance company that the owners of the burned greenhouse hadn't had anything to do with starting the fire that destroyed it.

So far as the murder of the burglar was concerned, Benjamin couldn't see what he was going to say having any effect on what the police thought about that: his father had made sure they would never find out what the man had photographed.

He had to wait twenty minutes before the social worker showed up, but although he was impatient to get his piece said he wasn't worried any longer by the delay because he'd heard DI Le Page tell his sergeant he was going to keep things on hold until after he had found out what Benjamin wanted to say to him.

The social worker was female, and he thought she was surprisingly young and pretty, not the forbidding school-mistressy figure he'd been afraid of. He'd also been afraid she would make him feel like a child, but in fact she made him feel more grown-up than he usually did in company. When he was sitting beside her opposite the two policemen he was surprised to find himself glad she was there, her scent was nice and he liked the interested and sympathetic expression in her face and her soft voice telling him to take his time and say exactly what he wanted. The two policemen nodded as she spoke, and this time it didn't frighten him when the DS put a tape in and announced the beginning of the interview.

"Off you go then, Benjamin," DS Mahy said then.

For a moment he thought he was going to blurt it straight out, but he managed to hold back and begin as he had been working out in his mind he should ever since he had woken up that morning. "It was when Mr Thomas came to dinner, and my father told him he'd decided to sell the pictures." He remembered that sunny evening in the greenhouse so horribly well. His mother had cooked an especially good meal and both his father and Mr Thomas had said things funny enough to make him laugh. But although he'd enjoyed himself, he'd started hoping during coffee that the grown-ups would decide to go into the house so that he could reclaim his space for himself for an hour or so before he was sent off to bed. When they walked away from the table he'd clear it in ten minutes and bring his things out of the small cupboard next to the big one where the pictures were kept. But then his father had mentioned the pictures . . .

"My father told Mr Thomas he was going to sell the pictures, and Mr Thomas started looking uncomfortable. Then he said he didn't think the pictures were what my parents thought they were, he believed they were nineteenth-century fakes." He could still see, in vivid detail, how his parents' faces had looked when Mr Thomas had said that.

The DI was moving restlessly in his chair, and Benjamin realised that up to now he had told the policemen only what they already knew. "Mr Thomas left earlier than usual," he said swiftly. "After he'd seen him out my Dad came back into the greenhouse and we went on sitting round the table. My Dad said that if Mr Thomas was right he wouldn't get the money he'd been hoping for from the sale of the pictures, and we wouldn't be able to expand the Golden Rose, we might even have to close it down." A horrid little worm of doubt had begun wriggling about in Benjamin's mind, making him wonder if he could be damaging rather than helping his mother and father by what he was saying, but he'd started now, he'd have to go on. "Then he said in a jokey way – it was only a joke, Mr Le Page – he said that if the greenhouse burned down we'd be all right, we had the certificates of authentication that had come with the pictures when my uncle left them to us, and they'd mean more to the insurance company than anything Henry Thomas might say. Then he said let's be serious and that they must make an appointment to have the pictures valued by a professional expert before putting them on the market, that was the only thing they could do." The worm was wriggling more strongly, and Benjamin was suddenly terrified by what he was doing. It was as crazy, as ill-thought-out, as what he had done before. "The only thing they could do," he repeated loudly. "That's what my father said, Mr Le Page, he wasn't thinking of doing anything else. And the next morning he made the appointment." Benjamin paused, to try and pull himself together and not give in to the dizziness which had suddenly come over him. He wanted to pull back from the table and put his head between his knees, but savagely he resisted.

"Go on, Benjamin," the lady beside him urged gently, patting his hand.

"Thanks," he muttered, and to his infinite relief was suddenly clear-headed. "My father'd told me off once, Inspector Le Page, for leaving a magnifying glass over some paper on the table in the greenhouse. He said it might catch fire. So I thought that if I lit a piece of paper deliberately it would seem as if the glass had started the fire. I had to have a hot sunny day, and it had to be when we were closed and going out, and two days before the appointment with the art expert it was both. So after breakfast I put the magnifying glass where my father had told me not to put it, and just before we were going out, about twelve noon I think, I went back there. The glass had made the paper very hot but it hadn't caught fire, and I lit a corner of it before locking the greenhouse up again as we always did, with the pictures being there, and slipped the key back on its hook in the house and then went out with my parents. Mr Le Page . . ."

To his further horror, Benjamin found that he was crying, great racking sobs that made it difficult to speak. The social worker asked for a break, but he was so keen to get it over he managed to say – to shout – that it was all right, he wanted to go on.

"When we got back," Benjamin said between hiccups, "the fire engine was there but the greenhouse was almost gone. The cupboard was all gone, with the pictures. Oh!" His wail of anguish was far too big for the small room. "I'd forgotten about the certificates, Mr Le Page, I'd forgotten they were in the cupboard with the pictures. If my father'd set fire to the greenhouse, he wouldn't have forgotten that, he'd have taken them away. So you've got to believe me, Mr Le Page, Mr Mahy" – Benjamin turned to meet the lady's kindly gaze, but he couldn't remember what they'd told him she was called – "my father had nothing to do with it, it was me. I'm telling you the truth!"

His outburst received the short silence its impact deserved. Then the DI said, "Did you tell your father and mother what you'd done, Benjamin?"

Tossing and turning in his bed that night, Benjamin knew he should say no, that his orgy of truthfulness should stop

there, but now it was an uncheckable avalanche. So he told
the policemen that he'd managed not to tell them right away
but in the end he hadn't been able to help it.

"So why didn't they tell the insurance company, Benjamin?"

"Because they knew that if they did I'd be taken away from
them! It was nothing to do with the value of the pictures. Oh,
don't you *see*?" How could they be sitting, all three of them,
so obviously not seeing? "I'm only twelve, a doctor told my
parents once that I'm maladjusted because I'm happy with
my own company, I don't play games unless I'm forced to,
and I'd rather be with older people than children of my own
age. If they'd told anyone how the fire started I'd be a fire
raiser too. My parents knew I'd be taken away from them,
not just for whatever time a sentence for fire-raising brings.
They knew I'd be called dangerously disturbed and that I
mightn't be allowed back with them for years. So of course
they didn't tell the insurance company. Didn't tell *anyone*.
How could they?"

"I understand what you're saying Benjamin," the DI at last
responded, quietly. "But do *you* understand – what you're
doing to yourself by telling me all this?"

"I don't care what happens to *me*!" Benjamin heard himself
shout passionately, although his insides were like jelly with
panic as he thought of the future he had just brought on
himself.

Detective Inspector Le Page turned to the social worker.
"Can you stay with Benjamin for the moment? Have a chat?
We'll find somewhere more cheerful for you to sit."

"Of course," she said, turning to smile reassuringly at
Benjamin. He still thought she was nice, but in the new icy
world which he had entered of his own free will it didn't
seem to matter any more whether she – or anyone else apart

from his mother and father – was nice or nasty. "Let's go, shall we, Benjamin?"

He mumbled agreement, and they followed the detectives out of the room and along the corridor. Benjamin had the odd sensation that he was floating along, that his feet weren't quite touching the ground, and at one point he pinched his thigh in the sudden desperate hope that he was asleep in bed and could wake up and find that the choice was still with him to leave well alone. But nothing happened, he was still following policemen along a corridor the way he'd be following other people in uniform along corridors for years and years into the future.

It was so awful he couldn't really think about it. The DS showed him and the social worker into a room with upholstered chairs, a television set – switched off – and a low table, said they would soon be back, and disappeared. Benjamin's legs went weak as the door closed, and the social worker helped him across the room to the brown sofa and sat him down beside her.

"I'm Miss Curley," she said, "in case you didn't catch my name the first time. It's an odd name, isn't it?"

Benjamin agreed that it was.

"Fortunately I had curly hair as a little girl or I might have been teased rather, don't you think?"

"You could have been," Benjamin said. He was amazed that he had been able to detach himself from the nightmare for a moment, long enough to consider Miss Curley's question and decide he agreed with what she had suggested.

"What made you come in and speak to Mr Le Page?" Miss Curley asked him.

"It was because I didn't want my Mum and Dad to lose the

insurance money for the pictures for something they hadn't done. For something I'd done."

"They could have told Mr Le Page themselves, Benjamin," she said, taking his hand. "But they preferred to keep you out of trouble than to have the money."

She had turned the worm of doubt into a snake, twisting through every corner of his brain. "Don't say that!" he shouted, pulling his hand away and leaping to his feet. "They shouldn't! They mustn't! They love the Golden Rose and I wanted them to be able to make it bigger and not have to worry about money. I wanted them to be *happy*!"

"Oh, Benjamin." She reached up to take his hand again, and eventually, sulkily, he let her have it and slumped back beside her. "No money could make up for them being without you. And you'll have to go away from them for a time now, you know."

"I know. I'd thought of that." But not properly. Not imagining how he would feel when he'd made sure it would happen.

"Both you and your parents have been very loving and unselfish to one another," Miss Curley said. "Your parents kept your secret for your sake, and you gave it away for theirs." He saw her face cloud. She couldn't believe, any more than he could, now, that what he had done could help them. "You must think of that all the time, Benjamin," Miss Curley went on insistently. "All the time, through whatever happens. You love one another, and that will make it all right in the end."

There was no answer he could give her and she didn't seem to expect one, she sat back in her seat and went on holding his hand in a silence he found surprisingly comforting.

When Tim and his DS reached Tim's office they stood a

few moments in silence too, but questioning each other with their eyes. Then Tim sighed, and Ted said, "Poor little sod. He's shot the three of them down with one bullet. That's it, isn't it, sir?"

"It has to be, sergeant."

But as Tim flopped into his chair he failed to experience the lightness of heart, the sense of a pattern being completed, which always accompanied the solving of a case. Perhaps it was because, in this case, a child was involved, a child who had just ensured his removal from his family. Perhaps that was all it was. It was enough.

"The child's just given the father the strongest motive for murder I've ever encountered," DS Mahy was continuing as he straddled a chair the wrong way and rested his arms on the back. "To say nothing of the one Charters already had, to get hold of enough money to ensure his future."

"Yes." Tim was back on his feet. "The boy must be detained for his own protection as well as for what he says he's done. He seems to be getting on well with Miss Curley. Let's leave them together and get someone here to contact the social workers and arrange accommodation for him."

"I'll see to it. Better take a WPC with us to leave with Mrs Charters, she'll have neither husband nor son tonight."

"Of course, Ted." He should have thought of it. "I'll get the warrant."

They filled the WPC in on the way to the Golden Rose. Bernard Charters opened the door to them and stood mutely questioning.

"This is WPC Gallienne," Tim told him. "Benjamin came to the station to see me. In view of what he told me we must keep him there for the time being and I thought your wife—"

"She has me."

"Ah," Ted said. "May we come in?"

Mute again, Bernard Charters stood aside. In the hall Tim came straight to the point.

"Bernard Charters," he said, "I am arresting you for the murder of Simon Shaw on the night of Tuesday, 7th August, in the Rue de Glycine." He was aware of a cry from the staircase, and that the WPC was running up towards it, but he had to go on. "You do not have to say anything, but it may harm your defence if you do not mention when questioned something which you later rely on in court. Anything you do say may be given in evidence."

There was a raging fury in Tim as he spoke, and he had expected to have difficulty restraining himself from putting his hands round Bernard Charters' neck and squeezing the life out of him for having squeezed the life out of his brother.

But to his uneasy surprise he was unable to focus his fury on the man standing so defiantly before him, head thrown back and eyes blazing with a fury of his own.

Fifteen

Anna had found her morning at the practice so restorative she awoke the next day with the anxious hope that Lorna would again feel well enough to be left alone for a few hours.

It was wonderful, she thought gratefully as she stretched relaxed limbs beside a still sleeping Tim, to have nothing more vital to be anxious about. Except, of course, Tim's state of mind, and she had accepted that she would be anxious about that for a long time to come. He had arrived home the night before comparatively early, to tell her about Benjamin Charters' visit to the station and the subsequent arrest of his father for the murder of Simon. He had also told her – and she had seen for herself in his restlessness and the absence of the sense of achievement he normally radiated when he had successfully concluded a case – that for some reason he couldn't understand he didn't feel good about it.

"You mean you don't think he did it?"

"How can I think that?" He set his whisky glass down on the table by her chair. "He has to have done it. He denied it, of course, but they usually do. And with the boy in his innocence giving him a second motive of parental concern as well as his survival instincts, well . . ."

He had been on the floor at her feet, and this was the moment he had twisted round to face her and she had parted her knees. His eyes had come to rest at last, on hers, and she had known in that moment that he would not exclude her again. It was the best moment of their honeymoon. Of their relationship, perhaps.

"So what is it?"

"It's the craziest thing, darling. Hey!"

Whitby had somehow insinuated his large body between Tim and his wife, balancing for a precarious moment across her bisected lap. His decision that he had not made a sensible move coincided with Tim's friendly shove, and he landed heavily on Duffy, spread out beside Anna's chair. The dog leapt up with a ferocious burst of barking, but it was only a reflex from shock and within seconds Whitby was crouched in the curve of his stomach, washing him to sleep.

Anna repeated her question as the peace flowed back. "So – what is it, Tim?"

"It's . . . I didn't hate him, I didn't want to do to him what he did to Simon. I expected to want to kill whoever murdered Simon and – I didn't. I didn't even feel the anger I felt against the insurance man who sent Simon out that night. I didn't feel anything. Except a sort of dismay. But it has to be all right, Anna. It has to be. It's only that I don't understand myself."

"Revenge is a bit of a sickly diet. I discovered that once myself when I gave in to it." When her first real love had walked out on her. "You feel terrible."

"I couldn't give in to it. Because it wasn't there."

"Well . . . You just said the man had the two strongest motives in the world. And you had to be unhappy about the boy and what's to become of him."

"I suppose so. But I had no idea I was so nice, darling."

189

It wasn't a very good joke, and they smiled rather than laughed, but Anna felt it could have turned a page.

Tim asked how his mother was.

"She seems all right. She survived my absence this morning, most of which she said she spent under the tree. And rather to her disgust she's got interested in a couple of morning TV programmes. We took Duffy to L'Ancresse again this afternoon and ate ice-creams in the car. Lorna still managed quite a good dinner, and she seemed ready for sleep when I left her about an hour ago. But Tim . . . It's not going to be as easy as that." *For you, either.*

"I know. I shan't be surprised if she wants to go home soon. And if she never wants to come back. Oh, Anna . . ."

She'd cradled his head for a while, and then they had gone up to bed and made love. Tim's stomach had started rumbling in the small hours, and he had answered Anna's whispered query with another surprised negative. So she had gone downstairs and made him a sandwich and both of them mugs of coffee and they had had them in bed and let the animals into the room as a rare indulgence (which meant on to the bed for Whitby under Duffy's forlorn gaze) before falling asleep again in each other's arms.

It was strange but nice to have Tim getting up for work reluctantly, no longer driven by his demon. But he was still early, and it was only nine o'clock by the time Anna had tidied around and was carrying a breakfast tray in to Lorna.

She was glad to see that her mother-in-law was asleep, her face touchingly young in the innocence of unconsciousness. As she drew the curtains back and stood looking down the garden, where the grass despite the sunshine was still heavily bedewed with the foretaste of autumn, Anna heard her move and sigh, and when she turned back to the bed Lorna was

190

struggling upright, her eyes on the tray Anna had put down on the bedside table.

"Dear Anna . . . You spoil me."

"I don't think so." Anna put the tray across Lorna's knees. "How are you?"

"Aches and pains are much better. Except for the one in my heart. But I don't want to lose that one, Anna. I don't want to forget."

"You won't." Anna took the napkin out of its ring, spread it over the sheet in front of the tray. "You don't. What you do is find one day that you're living with it, not just existing the way you did at first."

"Oh, you're such a help!" Lorna's elegant freckled hand caught Anna's and squeezed it. "You'll go to work again this morning, won't you? All day if you feel—"

"This morning, yes." What Anna felt was a surge of relief. "The afternoon's for you."

"Lovely!" Lorna tensed like a child anticipating a treat, bringing her hands up under her chin and squeezing her elbows into her sides. "Can we go out again?"

"Of course." Anna poured tea. "Now, I'll get ready for work, then I'll help you dress and go downstairs."

"Not this morning. I can manage, and I've got to be independent." Lorna hesitated, a piece of toast in her hand. "I must go home soon, Anna. Pick up my life. Be with Gina. I'm almost ready."

"Yes. Tim said last night he thought you might be. Lorna . . ." Anna perched on the bed. "He's arrested Bernard Charters for Simon's murder. Apparently his son undertook a bit of private enterprise: he set fire to the greenhouse when the value of the pictures was called in question, so that his father, he said, could collect the insurance money and carry

191

out his plans to extend the Golden Rose. The poor boy came in to confess to Tim off his own bat, without telling his parents, obviously not realising he was sealing his father's fate when he told Tim he'd confessed to him as well. So the father would have known that his son would be taken away from them if what he'd done ever came to light. Which Tim said gives him two of the strongest motives in the world for murder. We don't know what Simon photographed, but it must have been something that would have shown up one of the motives, and with Simon's blood on his sleeves . . ." Lorna knew about the blood, and all she did now was to put the toast in her hand back on to the plate. "He looked in to tell you himself last night but you were asleep."

Lorna drained her cup, then pushed the tray down the bed. "I'm glad I've never met him," she whispered. "Tim will have had to restrain himself, but I doubt I could have done."

"Yes . . ." Anna had told Lorna the facts. She would let Tim interpret them *vis-à-vis* himself, if he wanted to. "So it's finished. And that poor boy will be taken away from his parents."

"The father doesn't deserve a son, but for the boy and his mother . . . I can't take them on board as well, Anna," Lorna said, suddenly brisk and decisive in a way Anna already found characteristic. "Now, I'm going to get up. You just get yourself ready and go."

"I will." Anna got to her feet and picked up the tray. "I'll be back about one to make us some lunch. It's another lovely day and I'll put the cushions on the garden chairs before I go."

It *was* a lovely day, but somehow Lorna couldn't relax into it. She tried the garden, then came in to watch TV, then switched off and went into the kitchen to make herself a coffee. It really was time to go home, she thought as she carried the mug back into the sitting-room, put it down on the low centre table, and picked up the paper as she flopped on to the sofa. She'd ring Gina before the morning was out and tell her she'd soon be back. After the police had released Simon's body and they'd been able to give him a funeral. Which they would surely do soon, now that they'd found his killer. He wasn't a Le Page so he wouldn't be buried in the family plot in Candie Cemetery, where her nephew had been buried last year after *he* had been murdered . . .

She was glad Simon wouldn't be going to Candie. It was a dark, oppressive place even on a sunny day, and wasn't used any more except by old families who still had a space or two waiting in their piece of ground. She'd have to ask Gina if Simon had ever said what he wanted, but if Gina didn't know, and hadn't any strong feelings, she'd suggest burial at Foulon, the modern cemetery; she'd like him to end in Guernsey, to feel he was lying in the place of her birth . . . She was weeping when the telephone rang. It was a welcome diversion, and she found herself absurdly anxious that the caller might hang up before she was able to get her feet to the floor and cross to Tim's chair. But when she reached it the phone was still ringing. The caller was a woman with a Scots accent, who asked for Mrs Le Page.

"I'm Mrs Le Page," Lorna said. "But I expect you want my daughter-in-law, Mrs Anna Le Page."

"Mrs Anna Le Page, that's right," the caller said. "Could I please speak to her?"

"I'm afraid she's at work. If it's urgent you can ring her at—"

"It isn't urgent. Could you tell me if she'll be at home later?"

"Anytime after one o'clock, she told me. Can I help at all? Would you like her to ring you?"

"No, thanks." There was a pause. "I don't suppose Mr Le Page is there?"

"He's at work too, I'm afraid. I don't expect him back till this evening."

"Thanks. I'll ring again later. Cheers."

Lorna switched the TV on, and went listlessly back to the sofa. Her sorrow felt like a physical weight and made moving about an effort. Another episode was being shown of the programme she had half enjoyed the day before, but today it failed to involve her. She tried the other stations with no better result, and had just switched off when the telephone rang again.

"Wait, wait!" she yelled, launching herself across the carpet so eagerly she almost fell over the corner of a rug. Sobered, she carried on carefully to Tim's chair and made herself sit down before picking up the receiver.

This time the caller was a man, and asked for Mrs Lorna Le Page.

"Speaking!" she responded eagerly.

"This is Detective Constable Falla," the voice said. It sounded young. "Your son has asked me to ring you, Mrs Le Page. He'd like to meet you as soon as possible at the house of Mrs Constance Lorimer, and he's sending a car for you. He thought you might welcome ten minutes or so to get ready."

"What's happened? What's wrong?" Her heart was thudding so hard she wondered if the man would hear it.

"Nothing's wrong, Mrs Le Page! I'm sorry, I should have said that right away. It's just that your son has some further evidence and he thought you might like . . . But if you don't feel—"

"Of course I'll come! *And* I'll be ready in ten minutes!"

"Good. I'm to collect you myself. Detective Constable Falla."

Transformed, Lorna made herself climb the steep stairs sedately, looked critically at herself in her bedroom mirror, decided she would do, collected bag and jacket, and came down again. The cat was out, but she told a hopeful-eyed Duffy that she wouldn't be long. She saw the car from the window precisely ten minutes from the time of the phone call. It wasn't a police car, and the young man who had hared up the path had his ID in his hand.

"I thought you'd better see this, Mrs Le Page," he said, smiling at her. "Seeing that I've come in my own car. All the station cars were in use when I left and your son said—"

Lorna glanced at it. "That's all right, Constable."

She preceded him down the short path to the gate, which he shut behind them, got into the front passenger seat when he opened the door for her.

Constance Lorimer's! So Tim must have solved the mystery of the first attack as well. His success in finding Simon's murderer hadn't shaken her conviction that the hit-and-run in L'Hyvreuse had been directed against her, and now he must have obtained proof of it and wanted her to be there when he accused Constance.

Lorna was so excited she couldn't stop herself chatting to the DC, telling him she was a Guern and how beautiful the island was looking. He didn't say much in response, but he was half smiling and he had a lovely profile . . .

They were stopping outside Beth Smith's.

"I'm afraid you've got the wrong house," Lorna said. "This is where Mrs Lorimer's friend Miss Smith lives, Mrs Lorimer is at the other end—"

"I'm sorry, Mrs Le Page, I should have told you there's a slight change of plan." The lovely profile became a full face and the DC gave her a full, a dazzling, smile. "Your son is going to rendezvous with you here."

"Well, fine." Lorna shrugged. The prospect of the interior of Beth Smith's house was infinitely more attractive than the prospect of the interior of Constance Lorimer's. Not that she had ever visited Beth Smith, but Lorna could usually tell from a woman's appearance what her house was like.

Detective Constable Falla helped her out of the car and preceded her up the neat path. Lorna was admiring the layout and condition of the front garden when Beth Smith appeared at her front door, smiling.

"Good morning, Mrs Le Page! Do please come in. Your son isn't here yet, but he's just been on the telephone and we're to expect him at any minute. Would you like some coffee while we're waiting? The kettle's boiled."

"Thank you, I'd love some."

"Good. Will you take Mrs Le Page into the sitting-room, Constable, and I'll bring the coffee through?"

Miss Smith indicated an open doorway, and Lorna and the policeman went into a room of much the same dimensions as Constance Lorimer's, but so different Lorna found herself openly smiling at the delightful contrast. This room smelled sweet and sparkled with cleanliness, its decor was elegant and restrained, and it looked out on to another piece of beautifully tended garden.

"Nice place," the DC said.

"Lovely." Lorna noticed a spectacle case and a newspaper on the small table beside one of the fireside chairs, and sat down in the other. After a moment's pause the DC lowered himself gingerly on to the edge of the sofa, springing up again to take the coffee tray out of Beth Smith's hands and putting it down on the low centre table.

"Milk? Sugar?" Miss Smith enquired of them both.

When they were served, Lorna ventured to ask if Miss Smith was able to tell her the reason for the assembly at her house.

"Only that it's to do with poor Constance," Miss Smith replied, her smile tinged now with sadness.

"How kind you are!" Lorna said. "And this is delicious coffee." If a little strong.

"I'm glad you like it."

"I like your house too, Miss Smith. And your garden. Do you look after the garden yourself?"

Miss Smith told her that she had help with maintenance – mowing, edging and hedge-cutting – but that she enjoyed doing her own creative work, and the DC smiled down at his well-polished shoes, making Lorna suspect that maintenance man must be his own domestic role. She accepted a second cup of coffee from Miss Smith, and questioned Tim's lateness aloud as she started to drink it.

"Don't worry," the DC said. "It was one heck of a morning when I came out. I was glad to get away." Lorna had a vague idea that a look passed between him and Miss Smith. "He'll be here any minute," the DC said, his eyes returning to his shoes.

She was feeling vague altogether, Lorna realised as she set her cup down. Slightly drunk, she would have said if she'd been drinking alcohol. It wasn't a bad feeling, it was making her more and more relaxed and comfortable. It must be the cumulative effect of the pills she was still taking to ease the pain of her injuries.

"Are you all right, Mrs Le Page?" Beth Smith was asking.

"Yes. Yes, I'm fine." Lorna could feel her smile stretching beyond her own volition, and Miss Smith's face, also smiling, seemed to be less clearly visible than it had been when she arrived. That was true of the whole room, Lorna realised, as she looked from Miss Smith to the detective constable. She couldn't see his face very clearly, either, but she had the curious impression that he was suddenly serious. Very serious. It was all so strange Lorna gave a little laugh.

"Good," Miss Smith said. "Because I have a few things to say to you."

"Oh, yes?" Lorna settled herself firmly back in her chair, because of the odd sensation that if she didn't she might topple forward out of it. She didn't think she would take any more of those pills.

"Yes." Beth Smith turned to the detective constable. "I think she's ready," she said.

Lorna thought she saw the policeman shrug, get to his feet, cross the room and do something to a small box on a side table. Events had started to take a rather odd turn, but she wasn't worried because they felt no more real than events in a film being shown on a TV channel with interference, where you could only just make out the action and couldn't always be sure of the expressions on the actors' faces. She supposed she was involved in it, but it seemed an awfully long way away.

"Lorna Le Page!"

Beth Smith could have said it more than once. "I'm sorry." Lorna tried to concentrate. "I'm feeling a bit far away."

Miss Smith nodded. "As I expected. But I want you to listen to what I'm going to say to you, because I've been waiting to say it for thirty years. You didn't take Geoffrey

Lorimer away from his wife, you stupid woman, you took him away from *me*!"

"Wh-a-a-t?" She had listened, and as well as learning a terrible thing about Geoffrey she had also learned, as if she had know it all her life, that Tim wasn't coming and the man on the sofa wasn't a policeman. She had walked into a trap and she couldn't walk out of it because when she tried she couldn't even get to her feet.

Through the haze Beth Smith was nodding again. "That's right," she said. "You stay there, Lorna Le Page. And listen. When you met Geoffrey Lorimer he was already unfaithful to his wife. He and I were in love, passionately in love. It suited us to leave things as they were – I was only a few doors down from Constance and she didn't care where he was, didn't want to know so long as she had a comfortable chair and a packet of cigarettes. So she never knew, nobody ever knew, and I was happier than I'd ever believed possible."

"Must go . . ." Lorna mumbled. But somewhere else – she wasn't sure whether it was deep inside her or outside her helpless body and looking down on it – her mind had kept a clear place and was continuing to take in what Beth Smith was saying. Take it in with a horror as strong as her horror at being in the woman's power. Of being perhaps in the last hours – or moments – of her life.

"You can't go. Listen! Then *you* appeared, with your selfishness and your greed and your own husband, and you took him away from me. He didn't tell me he was going, but he told his wife. She and I were the merest of acquaintances then, and she didn't tell me because she was so stupid she didn't know he and I were more than acquaintances either. So *she* had a motive to drive her car at you where I didn't – then – and get stuck in a ditch for her pains. Oh, she really is a stupid woman, even stupider than you are. You thought you were the love of Geoffrey Lorimer's life, Lorna Le Page, that he'd remained faithful to a nightmare marriage until he met *you*! But I'm telling you now that he was no more than a miserable philanderer. If he hadn't died so soon after you took him away and wore him out, he'd have been on with the next one."

"N-o-o-o!" It took all Lorna's strength to give voice to the long-drawn-out whisper. But her outrage was so strong that for a moment it had taken over from her fear.

"Yes! It was after Geoffrey'd gone that I became friendly with Constance. I made all the overtures, because it was I who wanted it. It was the only way I could bear it, to be in the company of the other person Geoffrey had abandoned, the person to whom his desertion had done far more public harm. But far less private harm, of course. That was the wicked paradox, Lorna Le Page. Constance had nothing to get over, she'd let him go years ago. And I've never got over it at all. But outwardly Constance was the pathetic figure, the one people were sorry for. I at least was spared pity. To the world I was still a free spirit, elegant and enigmatic." The free part of Lorna's mind registered Miss Smith as an egotist even more monstrous than herself.

"Constance is so passive she accepted my overtures. She could take them or leave them, as she could take or leave anyone and almost anything else, but she soon discovered that I brought her advantages. She had Geoffrey's reluctant pittance, while I had a small fortune from my father. She didn't like driving – and her sight has become so bad she shouldn't be on the road – and I did. She didn't like cooking, but she liked eating the meals I made for her. She couldn't be bothered going to the cinema, but when I took her she

said how much better the films were on a big screen. And
so on. And when we learned you were coming back for your
son's wedding, Lorna Le Page, I was even able to persuade
her she was still angry. When we were outside St James and
saw the tall, fair young man standing beside you I told her he
was your toyboy and made her believe she was angry enough
to raise her fist. You saw it. And you smiled." Beth Smith
got to her feet and started to pace the room. Lorna found it
difficult to turn her head to follow her, but Beth was soon
back within her field of vision, standing in fact in front of
her, so close that Lorna could see the fury in her face.

"But I knew who he was, and I was the one who was
angry, Lorna Le Page! I was angry because of the worst
thing of all that you did. You presented me, on the steps of
St James, with Geoffrey as a young man. Had you forgotten
what he looked like while you were looking at other men?
Did it never occur to you that Constance might recognise
him? Weren't you afraid when she raised her fist? But it
wasn't Constance you had to be afraid of, Lorna Le Page,
it was me. Even if Constance had had real fire in her belly
she wouldn't have been able to see the young Geoffrey the
way I saw him – those beautiful eyes of hers couldn't see
detail the width of the forecourt. But my eyes could. And I
saw the son who ought to have been mine."

Beth Smith seemed to disappear, and it took Lorna a few
moments to realise that she had dropped back into her chair
the other side of the fireplace. She was aware of the dark
shape on the sofa moving and coughing.

"Geoffrey had made a promise to me, Lorna Le Page. A
promise which at the time he made it I believed he would
keep." Lorna was able to hear far more clearly than she was
able to see – didn't they say that hearing was the last faculty

201

to be lost when one was dying? – and Beth Smith's laugh was horrible. "He had promised me that if he gave me the baby I wanted he would leave Constance publicly and he and I would be married. I longed for that baby, Lorna, I yearned for it. Every month . . . But he gave it to you, and when it was thirty years old you showed it to me. I think that was the cruellest thing you ever did."

"But I didn't know . . ." Oh, how little she *had* known! "Beth . . . He gave me Simon because I was able to conceive him. If *you*'d been able—"

She had said the wrong thing. Beth Smith was standing over her again, and this time her arm was raised. Lorna knew, somewhere far off, that it was only because the man on the sofa shouted, "No!" that Beth didn't strike her.

"I can't wait any longer," Beth said, turning away from Lorna and moving towards the sofa.

"You better had, Beth," the man said, getting to his feet. "You don't want the police to find another dead body."

"The police . . . The police won't be coming!"

"I'm afraid they will."

"But we agreed . . . You'd ring the Le Page house from a call-box! To cancel the 1471!"

"I did make a call-box call, sweetheart. I rang the police in case someone else rang the Le Page house after I did and the 1471 didn't work."

Beth Smith let out a dreadful sound, half snarl, half wail, and Lorna thought she saw her raise her arm again. But the man caught it and twisted it behind her back, and the sound shrank to a yelp of pain.

"You thought you could buy me, Beth," he panted as he forced her towards the sofa. "And I thought so, too. But when it came to murder I found you couldn't. It's gone far enough. Too far."

"You fool!" She had managed to turn her head so that she was looking up into his face. "It was going so well! They'd have arrested the fellow from the Golden Rose. And no one would have known Mrs Le Page had been brought here before she disappeared." Suddenly she was limp. "Alan, you love me, you can't live without me, tell me you're joking, tell me—"

"I'm not joking. And I can hear a car."

Beth Smith screamed, and tried to bite him. Lorna wished dreamily that she could help the young man to subdue her, but he seemed to be managing all right on his own. He had her full length and face down on the sofa by the time Tim and DS Mahy came into the room.

Sixteen

"**B**ut how did you get in?" Lorna asked, she didn't know how much later. All she knew was that the rocking, retching zoom through space which had been the aftermath of her visit to Beth Smith had at last come to an end, and she was lying, relaxed and comfortable, in the guest bed in Rouge Rue with Tim and Anna to each side of her.

"We found the front door open," Tim told her. "Beth Smith's toyboy had left it for us, he told us later at the station."

"He had a lovely profile. Constance . . ."

"As innocent as the day. Innocent of any insight, any ability to read other people, if everything Beth Smith has said is to be believed."

Something unsatisfactory had started nudging at the back of Lorna's mind, and she suddenly knew what it was.

"I can only remember here and there what she said." She tried to struggle to a sitting position, but Tim held her gently down. "It's like a film that keeps fading out so that you can't follow it properly. I'm sorry, darlings."

"I'm surprised you remember anything, you were so power-fully tranquillised. But don't worry. Beth Smith had been waiting three decades for her grand confrontation, and she wasn't going to let it pass unrecorded. Her toyboy had his orders to switch a tape on when she started in on you."

"I think I saw him do it, but I didn't understand . . . Was it Beth or her man who drove at me in L'Hyvreuse?"

"It was Beth. He's aided and abetted, but that's as far as he's gone. Beth misread him, or thought her influence over him was a lot stronger than it was. When she told him what she'd done to Simon he'd had enough. And he appears to feel bad about setting Simon up. He was following him on Beth's instructions the second time he went to the Golden Rose, and he listened in to the call Simon made on his mobile to the London office of the insurance company. He says he was only a hedge-width away, and heard Simon agree to go in that night. We know from Ian Taylor of the London office that that's what Simon *did* agree. But only if he could enter without breaking, which I'm glad about, although what the hell does it matter now?" Lorna murmured a protest, and he took her hand as he went on. "Alan Hart – the toyboy – reported to Beth as ordered, and she told us herself that she parked in L'Hyvreuse that night and followed Simon when he left the Duke of Richmond. She knew where he was going, so I assume she kept far enough behind for Simon not to be aware he was being followed. She said she went straight to the forecourt of the Golden Rose and parked among the few other cars there. She didn't see Simon's car, but she'd hardly expected him to drive in and only had a short wait before he appeared on foot. She stayed there until he reappeared, gave him a few moments, then drove out into the lane – and we know the rest. She also told us . . ." Tim hesitated, looking gravely into his mother's eyes.

"Told you what, Tim?" she whispered. "Please go on."

"She told us it was seeing his father's face again, so clear and close under the lamps by the gate, that made her run him down. Up till then she hadn't known what she was going to do, if anything. I think the shock of seeing Simon for the first time on the steps of St James and recognising his father in him had sent her over the edge. Well, she'd already tried to run you down. She'd never come to terms with Lorimer's desertion, and when she discovered after thirty years that he'd given the child he'd promised her to someone else . . ."

Anna as well as Tim was now looking at her with a sorrow of such gravity Lorna felt she owed it to them to explain how she felt about Geoffrey's wretched deception.

"Listen," she said, and this time Tim let her sit upright. "Your father was a good man, Tim."

"My father . . . ?"

She could see apprehension joining the sadness in their two faces, and had to suppress a giggle as she suspected them of wondering if her experience had turned her brain. "No," she assured them. "I haven't gone mad too. It's just that there's something I have to say. When I deserted your father, Tim, I took with me a burden of guilt I've never shed. And never wanted to shed, because I've a puritan conscience buried in me somewhere and I felt it was my just punishment. When I took Geoffrey away, I thought from Constance" – she saw them exchange a brief relieved smile as they noticed the rueful twist she could feel on her own lips – "that burden was doubled. I'd injured two good men. Geoffrey's near-perfection combined with your father's total goodness was very hard to live up to – even harder, somehow, when they had both died and could never do anything to dim their pristine images." Lorna felt her self-mocking smile again, then the solemnity of her face as she looked from one to the other of them, knowing how important it was to her to define correctly what her new knowledge of Geoffrey had done to her memory of him. "It's funny, Tim," she heard herself saying. "If I'd ever discovered your father was less than an honourable man I'd have felt the whole world had crumbled. Discovering that Geoffrey was less than honourable . . . I'm feeling *relieved*. As if I've shed a load."

"Perhaps your subconscious suspected he wasn't worth it," Anna suggested.

"I don't know. Perhaps I disguised my lust as esteem to make myself feel better about what I was doing. But Tim . . ." Lorna seized his arm. "In the end, it's your father who's with me. Geoffrey's gone, he dissolved in those few moments Beth told me about him, and I'm more sure by the minute that I'm happy to let him go. Now I can mourn what I did to your father. And feel like his wife again. Does that make you angry, darling?"

"Of course not. It makes me glad." For the second time Tim hesitated. "But don't be too hard on Geoffrey. He was Simon's father."

"Yes. But Simon should have been Beth's." It was extra-ordinary how clear everything had suddenly become to her. The sunshine filling the simple, white-walled room seemed like the expression of the clarity with which she was seeing the past, the present, and even the future "If she could have conceived, everything would have been different. I would have stayed with your father, and Beth would have been a normal, happy mother. Simon would have been different. But he'd have been alive."

"We can't be sure of any of that," Anna responded swiftly.

"We certainly can't be sure you'd have stayed with Father," Tim ventured. He knew it was a gamble which if it failed could cause damage to them all. But he also thought he knew his mother, and to his relief he was right: her tense face relaxed into a smile.

"No, we can't, darling. But we do know – because I know – that I've never ceased to honour him above all men. Oh, Tim . . ."

It was her most welcome weeping since Simon had died. When it was over Tim suggested that she sleep for an hour before the lunch one of them would bring up to her.

"Lunch!" Lorna had nestled down into the bed, but sprang up and seized his hand again. "But I thought . . . It was nearly lunchtime when I was at Beth's. How have you had time to talk to her and her toyboy? You have to mean supper, Tim, or I *am* going mad."

"You didn't have any lunch when you left Beth Smith's," Tim said. "And you had your supper last night by drip in the Princess Elizabeth. Shock, and Beth Smith's ministrations. But they let us bring you home for the night, and you've woken up in the middle of a sunny tomorrow morning."

"So I've lost a day and a night." Lorna fell back on her pillow, winded by a lesser but still highly disconcerting shock. "Well, I do seem to have been dreaming bad dreams for a long, long time. They're all I can remember since I saw you and that nice sergeant of yours coming through Beth Smith's sitting-room doorway."

"I saw you pass out. Alan Hart told me it was only tranquillisers, but we called an ambulance. How on earth did Hart persuade a policeman's mother to get into an unmarked car?"

Her embarrassed wriggle went the length of the bed. "He showed me an ID and I only glanced at it. I wouldn't have known exactly how it ought to look, anyway. I'm sorry, Tim."

"You're no different from the majority of the population. I suspect Alan Hart has made capital out of that forgery a few times."

208

"He isn't a murderer, though," Lorna said. "And he saved my life."

"After putting it on the line. But yes, that will help him. Beth Smith's in hospital under police guard. I don't think there's a chance of her ever being at liberty again."

"A-a-a-h!" Lorna stretched her limbs and smiled from one to the other of them. "I will go to sleep now, darlings. So long as you promise to rebook your Scottish honeymoon. For the day after you book my flight to London."

"We'll try. But first, Mother . . . There'll be Simon's funeral."

They braced themselves for the pain of her remembering, and watched her wince and turn her head into the pillow.

"He seems so long gone, I forgot," she whispered.

"I wonder you haven't forgotten everything, with what Beth Smith did to you," Tim said rallyingly. "I should be able to find out this afternoon when he'll be released to us."

"I'll ring Gina," Lorna said. "Find out what she wants." She looked up at them, her eyes widening in surprise. "I've just remembered, I was going to do that when Beth Smith's boyfriend rang . . . Leave me now, will you, darlings."

Tim and Anna went downstairs and carried the chair cushions out to the garden.

"Are you going to work this afternoon?" Tim asked her, as they tied them on.

"I'm staying with Lorna. I gather you're working."

"I must. And I want to call on Bernard Charters, I wasn't around when he was released last night. When we withdrew the murder charge he admitted to the theft of the film in Simon's camera, but said he'd immediately destroyed it. I left it at that, but there are one or two things I'd like to know." As he caught Anna's eye Tim's gravity dissolved

209

into a reminiscent smile. "Last night was so marvellous, darling, I'm the proverbial giant refreshed. Hey, there!" Two gorgeously overblown rose bushes were agitating and, as they watched, Whitby emerged on to the ragged edge of the lawn in a shower of petals. Tim turned back to Anna with a grin. "How about an hour with the secateurs and the shears?"

He had no need to visit the Charters again, the Chief would express the regret of the Guernsey police force at Bernard Charters' brief wrongful imprisonment, and he would see him when he was brought to court for withholding vital evidence in a murder case and for robbing a corpse. For the moment Charters was free on police bail, but was due before the magistrates in two days' time. Tim was sure he would escape with a fine, and there would be no charge against him with regard to the fire: that remained a matter between him and his insurance company, with the additional factor of his son's involvement . . .

The Golden Rose was still closed for business, and Tim drove reluctantly across the empty expanse of the forecourt, round the building beyond the deserted sales area, and drew up outside the private house.

He had not wanted to see Marjorie Charters but she came to the door, looking so weak and haggard he put an instinctive hand out towards her.

She recoiled from it as if on a reflex. "What is it now?" she asked wearily.

"A private visit. To say how sorry I am about it all. About – about the night you spent alone."

"The worst night of my life," she said matter-of-factly.

"It has to have been. May I see your husband?"

"And ask him if he'd care to tie up a few loose ends?" The

question was cynical, but Marjorie Charters asked it flatly, as if she was merely corroborating the inevitable. He realised that the tension had gone out of her.

"I *would* be grateful personally, if he felt he could, Mrs Charters. Is he in?"

"He's in, Mr Le Page. You'd better come in, too." She pulled the door wider, and stood aside.

Bernard Charters was in his study, sitting at the knee-hole desk and staring into space. Tim saw him as they were crossing the hall, but by the time they reached the room he was on his feet and asking Tim to sit down. His wife closed the door on them.

"I'm so very sorry," Tim heard himself saying as he took the armchair Charters indicated. "It must have been very hard for you and your wife, knowing the truth about the fire but feeling unable to reveal it because of your son's involvement." He hoped he had summed up the cruelty of their dilemma at the same time as letting Charters know that he understood there had been one.

"It was, Mr Le Page. It still is. We're gutted." But for him, too, the tension had gone.

"Benjamin . . . ?"

"They're allowing him home at night. For the time being and subject to my undertaking to keep him under constant surveillance. During the day he's to attend the Princess Elizabeth to be assessed for a report, he's there now. No one would tell me what will happen to him eventually."

"I expect because they don't know. I doubt they've had to deal with anything like this before. But I'm glad to hear he's sleeping at home." Tim shifted in his seat. "Mr Charters, I can't believe you destroyed the film you took from Simon Shaw without looking at it. Are you prepared to tell me what it was that he had photographed? I'm asking you unofficially, for my own information." For his own need to know every least thing still left to be learned about his brother. "If you'd like it put on record as part of your defence against stealing the film, then of course you can add it to your statement. But for now . . ."

Charters shrugged, got to his feet, and walked over to the window, where he stood with his back to Tim, looking out on the small courtyard garden. "He hit the jackpot," he said. "If I'd been put on trial for his murder I'd never have told you. But it doesn't matter now. He'd photographed the confession my son had made to having started the fire, and how he'd done it. Benjamin didn't tell either his mother or me for several days. We knew something was wrong, but it was easy to put it down to his distress over the loss of the greenhouse and the pictures. He started having nightmares and crying out, he wasn't eating, and then he appeared with a couple of sheets of paper and broke down as he handed them over. I put the confession into that drawer." Charters indicated the bottom right-hand drawer of the knee-hole desk. "After the break-in I went straight to it, and although it was still there I felt sure my burglar had obtained his evidence. It was then that I heard the car, and of course I thought it was him driving off. I don't know what made me go out into the lane – I think I just had to do something, I was in such anguish, learning in one dreadful moment that the fraud I had tried to commit to save my son would be exposed, and my son would be lost. I found the man dead in the hedge, and took the film as I said in the statement I made last night. I destroyed it immediately I'd looked at it, and knowing you'd come with a search warrant I mailed Benjamin's confession to myself at the house in Italy I inherited from my brother along with the pictures. I put 'To await arrival' in Italian on the envelope, so it will no doubt be lying now on the mat inside the front door."

"Will you go and collect it?"

Charters turned from the window with another shrug, and came back to his chair smiling. "Will I be allowed to?"

"I should say so. If not while your case is pending. What will you do in the long term?"

"Cut my losses. Sell up and go back to England. That's where Benjamin will surely be sent, and Guernsey's too small to reabsorb us, we'll always be the wrong 'uns from the mainland."

"You may be right," Tim conceded. "I'm so very sorry."

Charters deep-set eyes appeared to be studying him. "I believe you are," he said eventually.

"So sorry," Tim went on, wondering if he had known earlier what he was now going to say, "that if you give me your word that you'll keep it to yourself and your wife I'll tell you something which may never be made public. And which I hope you'll feel excuses me if at any time during the investigation I made you afraid that I'd lost my objectivity. Will you give me your word?"

"Of course."

"Thank you." But Tim hesitated a moment before going on. "I know nothing about your burglar's business life, Mr Charters." It hurt him that this was barely a lie. "But he was my younger brother. That information is the one recompense I can give you."

Charters drew a deep breath, and to his amazement Tim was suddenly aware of his eyes because they were sparkling with tears. "I don't practise *schadenfreude*, Inspector Le Page, and it's no recompense to me to know that your loss is greater than mine; your secret shocks and grieves me. But I do very much appreciate that you've chosen to share it with me. And why." Charters got to his feet. "And now, if you will excuse me . . . I shall be in court as ordered."

It was in the nature of the man, Tim thought, to take what he was given and not ask for more.

"Of course. And if you decide to alter your statement, or add to it, please let me or my sergeant know."

Tim held out his hand, and Charters took it in a brief strong grasp. Out in the hall his wife took it more gingerly. She let him out without speaking.

He was glad the afternoon kept him busy with other things. When he got home his mother and Anna were reclining under the tree on another perfect early evening.

"We get Simon back tomorrow," he said at once, not sitting down. "Did you speak to Gina, Mother?"

"Yes. And she's happy about burial here at Foulon. She won't be coming. As soon as the funeral date's fixed, Tim, you must reinstate your third-time-lucky honeymoon."

"We will." He and Anna smiled at one another.

But he didn't want to sit under the tree with them, the way they'd sat the day his mother had arrived in Guernsey and he had so earnestly wished she had come alone. "I'm feeling short of exercise," he lied. "So I think I'll take Duffy for a run by the sea. I shan't be long."

How long he would be recovering from his brother's death Tim didn't know, but as he released the dog on to the springy turf of L'Ancresse and tried to keep pace with him, he knew he was running from his fear that he and his brother's killer might have one thing in common.